"Are you ready?" *walked through the archway*

This time she was modeling a deep cobalt-blue lingerie set. It showed skin, a lot of it. The garter belt gave her the look of a wanton, the G-string under it an invitation to sin. The bustier she wore on top made her slight curves look bountiful. And stopped just above her nipples, which stood out against the smooth fabric.

Desire thudded through Rand. He couldn't stop staring at her. He wanted his mouth on hers; he wanted to be inside her.

"What do you think?" Cilla asked.

Rand wasn't sure coherent thought was on the program. She looked like a naughty schoolgirl, amused with her own daring. She looked like a temptress accustomed to making strong men weak. She looked like a woman of flesh and blood and unapologetic appetites. And all he could do was feast right along with her.

"Come here," he ordered, because that was all he could handle....

Blaze™

Dear Reader,

Welcome back to the world of SEX & THE SUPPER CLUB. *Nothing but the Best* is Cilla's book, and boy, was it a blast to write. Years ago I read an interview with Larry McMurtry in which he described his characters as though they were real people with minds of their own, people he just tracked and listened to as they went through their lives. I thought it was fanciful at the time—then I started writing novels and discovered that it was absolutely true. Cilla knows exactly who she is and what should happen to her. It's when she runs into a stubborn, sexy guy named Rand that she gets into trouble.

Cilla's a feisty heroine who's great fun. I'd love to hear what you think of her. Drop me a line at kristin@kristinhardy.com. Look for more of SEX & THE SUPPER CLUB coming in the future— we still have to follow the stories of Paige, Thea and, best of all, Delaney. To keep track, sign up for my newsletter at www.kristinhardy.com for contests, recipes and updates on my recent and upcoming releases.

Have fun,

Kristin Hardy

Books by Kristin Hardy

HARLEQUIN BLAZE

*Under the Covers
**Sex & the Supper Club

NOTHING BUT THE BEST

Kristin Hardy

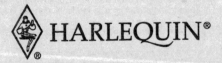

HARLEQUIN®

TORONTO • NEW YORK • LONDON
AMSTERDAM • PARIS • SYDNEY • HAMBURG
STOCKHOLM • ATHENS • TOKYO • MILAN • MADRID
PRAGUE • WARSAW • BUDAPEST • AUCKLAND

To Matt, Ernie and Bitsy,
the legendary basement gang,
and to Stephen, my favorite
person in the whole world.

ISBN 0-373-79168-2

NOTHING BUT THE BEST

Copyright © 2004 by Kristin Lewotsky.

This edition published by arrangement with Harlequin Books S.A.

® and TM are trademarks of the publisher. Trademarks indicated with
® are registered in the United States Patent and Trademark Office, the
Canadian Trade Marks Office and in other countries.

Visit us at www.eHarlequin.com

Printed in U.S.A.

Prologue

Los Angeles, 1996

"OKAY, EVERYONE, you can stop unpacking, dinner's here."

Cilla Danforth shut the front door with her elbow, balancing the stack of pizzas as she stared at the disordered living room of her new house. Despite the confusion that dotted the room, Cilla could still feel the warmth of her late grandmother's presence. No reading of the will changed that. But Gran had wanted her to have a home of her own. Cilla figured that she'd have understood that at twenty, Cilla wasn't ready to live alone yet. She wanted friends around her, roommates to share her days in the rambling Depression Modern home in the affluent neighborhood of Brentwood.

Cilla shook her head briskly and carried the stack of pizza boxes into the kitchen. Like magic, the scent drew the rest of her new roommates, the same way it did when they got it delivered to the university drama department when they were all working on a production.

"Trish, where's all the kitchen stuff you got at the store?" Kelly Vandervere yelled.

Trish ran down the stairs, her long red hair clubbed back in a braid. "Look on the counter behind you. I grabbed paper plates and napkins. I thought we could figure out what to do about real plates once we got settled. I don't think Cilla should have to buy everything. We're living here, too."

"Well, these will do for the time being," said Delaney, a gleam in her eye as she opened the box holding the pepperoni pizza.

They settled in the living room, sitting on the sofa or against the wall.

"One of the things we're going to have to get is enough places for all of us to sit," Cilla observed.

"I got a couple of upholstered chairs when they sold off the props from my dad's last movie," Sabrina Pantolini told them.

"That'll help," Cilla said. "Paige, you want to go to Danforth Home with me this week and help me pick out a couple of sofas?"

Paige's eyes lit up at the idea of a shopping spree at Danforth, Cilla's family's business and the most luxurious department store on Rodeo Drive. "Any time."

"Nothing too gorgeous, Paige," Thea begged. "I don't want nightmares from spilling wine when I'm making out with Rob Frieden, or something. Not that I'm planning to," she added hastily.

Sabrina winked. "Not planning to do what, spill wine or make out with him?"

"Spill wine, of course. As to Rob..." She gave a saucy look and took a bite of pizza.

Delaney raised her Coke. "Here's to escaping the dorms."

Trish shook her head. "Here's to Cilla, for inviting us to live in her new house."

"Thanks to you guys for being my roomies," Cilla countered. "We'll fix it all up, get it in great shape."

"Using lots of sexy contractors, I hope," Kelly added.

"My dad made sure it stayed fine structurally, but you'll see it needs paint and repairs. Toward the end, Gran just wasn't comfortable with anything changing, so some of the walls are pretty bad."

"I'll paint my room," Paige, always the designer, volunteered immediately. Even though she'd been hauling boxes all day with them, she looked as coolly blond and tidy as always.

"Our room," Thea reminded her.

"Trust me, darling, you'll love it," Paige assured her.

"So let's see," Delaney said thoughtfully. "We've got four bedrooms. Sabrina and Kelly, you're rooming together, and Trish and I, which leaves Cilla with the only private room."

"As appropriate," Trish pointed out. "She owns the place."

"So what if one of us has a boyfriend and wants to have some privacy?" Delaney asked.

"You mean when," Kelly said, rubbing her hands.

"It's a good thing you and Delaney didn't wind up in the same room. I don't know who would be fighting more, you or your hormones," Paige observed.

"Well, unless we figure something out, it's looking like Cilla's going to be the only one getting any action, here," Delaney replied.

"If you're good, I'll fill you all in on it," Cilla said with a smile. "Trust me."

1

The present....

THE HIGHWAY WAS open, the wind was in her hair, and for the first time in nearly two months, Cilla Danforth felt free. Around her, the California desert stretched out in all directions, flat and open and fringed with mountains. She turned up the stereo. Friday night and nowhere to be for two whole days.

It was almost better than sex.

Not that she had recent memory of that, of course. Running around to the spring collections in Paris, Milan and New York made it a little hard to have a social life. She was back in her own time zone now, though, at least for a few weeks. Yes, being couture buyer for Danforth's was exciting. And being the bridge-line buyer for the coast-to-coast Forth's chain was a challenge. Sometimes, though, she wanted to stop being Cilla Danforth, fashion guru and department store heiress, and just...be.

Cilla would cheerfully have kissed the administrative assistant who'd chosen the Carrington Palms Hot Springs Resort as the location for the Danforth Corporation strategic-planning meeting. The rest of the board and management was showing up Sunday night, or even Monday morning. That was practically an eternity away and she had every intention of spending that eternity by the pool.

And leaving Cilla Danforth behind for a couple of days.

The setting sun sent long fingers of shadow stretching out ahead of her as she headed east. The cars coming toward her—such as they were on this stretch of highway—had begun switching on their lights. Still, she was making good time, and barring unforeseen incidents, she'd make the resort before it got dark.

A sudden explosion made her jump. Instantly, the car began to slew on the highway. Fueled by a spurt of adrenaline, Cilla fought to brake and keep her little Porsche roadster heading straight. Finally, what seemed like eons later, she brought the car to a stop on the shoulder.

Then she dropped her head onto the steering wheel and waited for the shakes to go away.

Okay, triage. It had to have been a blowout. She just needed to confirm it, call AAA to send someone to change the flat, and she'd be on her way. It wasn't a disaster, just an inconvenient delay. She refused to let it interfere with her bliss.

Cilla slipped on her shoes, wishing she'd remembered to toss her driving moccasins back in the car after she'd worn them last. Stilettos and a miniskirt weren't exactly approved tire-changing attire, but then who planned for that sort of thing anyway?

Teetering a bit, she walked toward the back of the car. It didn't take much more than looking at the pieces of rubber littering the highway beyond to confirm that it was a blowout, but she glanced at the car anyway to see more rim than rubber showing on her left rear wheel. A muscle truck with chunky tires drove by, the two guys inside whooping and making enthusiastic suggestions about how she might spend her night.

Wasn't she just a lucky girl, she thought as she watched their taillights fade.

Cilla slipped back into the car and pulled out her cell phone. And, remembering the truck, she put up the top on the convertible, staring out at the purpling sky as the fabric canopy came down over her. It wasn't much, but in a place this desolate, every little bit helped.

"TWO HOURS?" Cilla repeated in astonishment.

"I'm sorry, ma'am," the phone operator responded, "but you're out in the middle of nowhere and the only tow companies we've got in the area are on calls. The first one who finishes will be out to take care of you."

The sun was dipping below the horizon. When Cilla looked out to either side, she saw only mesquite, sagebrush, the occasional tumbleweed. It had been wonderfully open and free when she'd been driving. Now, it was fast becoming merely empty and intimidating. She wasn't a woman who was daunted by much, but the last thing she wanted to do was sit by the side of the road for two hours while it turned dark.

"Ma'am? Did you want me to put you on the call sheet?"

Two hours, Cilla thought, plus the time for the driver to change her tire.

Unless she changed it herself.

After all, how hard could it be? She'd seen people change tires before, in the movies, anyway. Her owner's manual probably had directions. As she told her father regularly, she was capable of far more than anyone gave her credit for. Why be a girl and wait for a tow-truck driver to come bail her out? Self-sufficiency, that was the ticket.

"Ma'am?"

"Never mind," Cilla said firmly. "I'll take care of it."

Twenty minutes later, she stood cursing as she tried to get the lug nuts on the wheel to turn. The owner's manual made it sound simple: take off the lug nuts, jack up the car, pull off the old tire, put on the new and be on your way.

They just didn't warn you that the lug nuts had been tightened by the Incredible Hulk.

Putting her weight on the tire iron for what seemed like the hundredth time, Cilla gritted her teeth and shoved. It did exactly nothing, and stilettos weren't exactly the right footwear for stomping. She could feel the bruises forming on her palms. Maybe it was time to reconsider the tow truck, she thought as yet another car whisked by, stirring up dust. Bad enough she'd broken a fingernail loosening the wing nut that held the jack in place in the trunk, not to mention the fact that she'd yet to figure out just exactly where the jack was supposed to go when the time came to raise the car.

That part, of course, wasn't particularly important just then. If she couldn't get the lug nuts off, her experiment in tire changing was going to come to a screeching halt.

In time with her thoughts, she heard the chirp of tires

on pavement. Cilla whipped her head around toward the front of her convertible and froze. The car that had just passed her was on the shoulder about a quarter mile ahead, and swiftly backing up in her direction.

Her heart began to thud. Maybe—probably—it was a good Samaritan. Maybe it was some nice guy who'd be eager to help. She'd grown up in L.A., though, and was all too aware that there were other types of people who stopped for lone women broken down at the side of the road, especially out in the desert.

She picked up the tire iron and got back into the car. It never hurt to be cautious.

Brake lights glowed red as the car stopped a few feet in front of her. White, late model, American made. Didn't signify much of anything. Psychos could still drive Ferraris and Hummers, and perfectly decent people drove rolling junk heaps. The door of the car opened and she swallowed. Be prepared for anything, she told herself. The driver could be capable, clueless but well-intentioned, or up to no good.

Or, she thought in a moment of stupefied surprise, he could just be the most beautiful man she'd ever seen. Lean and lanky in jeans, he walked toward her in the wash of headlights, a sheaf of dark hair falling over his forehead. His face was all intriguing angles. His mouth looked soft and eminently kissable. If she'd met him in a cocktail bar, she'd have thought she'd died and gone to heaven.

But she wasn't in a cocktail bar.

He put a hand on her roof and bent down to look at her. "Need some help?"

Up close, he packed a punch. A five o'clock shadow

blued his jaw deliciously. His eyebrows drew sharp lines above his dark gray eyes. Who knew Samaritans were so gorgeous?

Of course, Ted Bundy had been good-looking and charming, too, she reminded herself, but she still brought the window down an inch. "No thanks. I've got a tow truck coming," she said, holding up her cell phone.

"It kind of looked like you were trying to change it yourself when I drove by. Are you sure you don't need a hand?"

She could think of a thing or two to do with hands like his, but not in her current situation. "It's nice of you to offer but I'm sure you're on your way somewhere." *And if conditions were different, I'd be happy to jump you.*

"I've got time," he said easily.

Cilla hesitated. Unless she got this stranger, or a tow-truck driver, to change the tire, she clearly wasn't going anywhere. Part of her was ready to open the door and take him up on his offer—how many Ted Bundys could there be? The other part of her, the part that had lived in the city for too long, perhaps, wasn't about to take a chance. "I appreciate the thought," she began, "but I'd really prefer to stay in here and wait for the tow-truck driver." *No matter how gorgeous you are.*

Instead of looking offended, he nodded. "You know what? You're being smart. That's exactly what I'd tell my kid sisters to do in your spot. But what's not smart is for you to be sitting on the side of the road out here in nowhere land." He gave her a thoughtful look. "How much do you weigh?"

"Pardon me?"

"Never mind. You look pretty small. How about if you stay put and I'll jack up the car with you in it?"

Cilla blinked. "Isn't that dangerous?"

A corner of his mouth curved up in a smile. "Not unless you plan to start bouncing around."

"Are you sure? I can wait for the tow-truck driver, or even do it myself."

His smile broadened. "I'm sure you could, but I bet I can do it quicker. I worked at a garage when I was in high school. And the quicker you say 'yes,' the quicker it'll be done." He paused, watching her. "The price is right," he wheedled. "I'll have you on the road in fifteen minutes."

Cilla gave up. "Okay, fine."

"Good call," he said approvingly. "Okay, let's get to it. Make sure it's in gear and put on the emergency brake. Then don't move until I tell you."

As he walked to the back of the car, Cilla leaned over and adjusted her side mirror to watch him. If he looked good from the front, he looked even better from the back. Not to mention the fact that he sounded like a genuinely decent guy. She felt the car shift as he pulled the tire out of her trunk. And then he was walking forward to knock at her window.

"What did you do with the tire iron?"

Cilla looked down and realized she was still holding it. She raised her hand.

He blinked and a down-to-his-toes belly laugh rolled out of him. "I see you're prepared. So much for worrying about a helpless woman at the side of the road."

"You should be careful about laughing at a person holding a lethal weapon," she said with dignity, her cheeks burning.

"Damned straight," he agreed. "Never mind, I'll get mine."

And that, of course, treated her to a direct view of him from behind. He rummaged in his trunk for a moment, bending down, she was pleased to see, before getting the crowbar. There was nothing quite like a fine-looking ass on a man, Cilla mused, small and tight and marble hard.

Back at her car, it took him approximately five seconds and one try on each to break loose the lug nuts. It was because she'd loosened them for him, she told herself, trying not to be impressed. The car lurched as he raised the jack, and then the old wheel was off and the spare put on so efficiently it seemed like only a minute or two had passed before the car was back down. There was something immensely sexy about a capable man. Her system buzzed pleasantly.

Sooner than she would have wanted, he was back by her window. "The jack is back in its bracket and I put the old tire in the well but you should get it fixed right away. This is bad country to be driving around in without a spare."

"Of course." Cilla hesitated, wanting to be more forthcoming and knowing it wasn't smart. "You've been unbelievably nice. How can I thank you?"

He shrugged. "Don't worry about it. I'm happy I was here to help." His eyes locked on hers and the seconds stretched out. "So, anyway, you're all set," he said finally, as though he really wanted to say something else. "You okay to drive? Do you want me to follow you for a while?"

"Um…" she said helplessly. Offering money seemed tacky. What she really wanted was to see him again, but she knew nothing about him, not who he was, not where he was going. *You've done well so far,* she told herself. *Don't screw up.*

As though he were reading her thoughts, he smiled faintly. "The way I look at it, what goes around comes around. It's your turn next. Keep an eye out and when you get a chance to do something good for someone, do it." He looked in her lap. "And you might want to put the tire iron back in your trunk after I leave."

He gave her a wave and walked back to his car. The last thing she saw was the red of his taillights fading slowly into the gathering darkness.

"CHECKING IN, name of Rand Mitchell." Rand slid his credit card on the marble counter.

A blond desk clerk, made up to within an inch of her life, beamed at him. "Welcome to the Carrington Palms Hot Springs Resort, sir. And how are you this evening?"

Considering he was going on his twenty-fifth hour without sleep, not too bad, Rand thought. "A little jet-lagged, but otherwise okay." Milan suddenly seemed a long time ago, but not very far away. With its curved marble archways and pillars, and cool tile on the floor, the lobby of the resort would have fit right in in Italy. To one side, an archway led into the vast glass-roofed central atrium of the resort, with its fountains and flora. If you didn't look up too high, you'd think you were outdoors, with the minivillas in the courtyard, the French doors and balconies up on the wall.

"Well, you've come to the right place if you want to relax," the clerk told him. "We've got a world-class golf course designed by Jack Nicklaus and ten outdoor mineral hot springs for you to relax in when you're done. And, of course, Palm Springs is only another half hour up the highway, if you want to get out and see the sights."

He'd already seen the best the desert had to offer, Rand reflected, flashing on the stranded motorist he'd stopped to help. He'd glimpsed her fighting with the tire as he'd driven past. Tired as he'd been, he couldn't help thinking about his mother or one of his sisters stuck on the side of the road in the middle of nowhere. Once he'd done that, stopping to help was a no-brainer.

Then he'd walked up and seen her triangular, tilty-eyed face, looking out at him from her absurd little roadster like a fox peeking out of a thicket. And suddenly being the chivalrous gent hadn't seemed like a hardship at all. The only thing that had been a hardship had been making himself drive away.

He shook his head faintly. Rand Mitchell liked women. A lot. He liked the way they looked, the way they felt, the way they thought, their sometimes quirky behavior and insecurities. He dated the same way he played in a local basketball league before he'd moved to Europe—with casual enjoyment, adeptness and no particular commitment. Serious wasn't for him; it never had been.

Done deal, he reminded himself as the clerk handed him his room folio. His mystery woman was probably a rich wife headed off to her estate in Palm Springs. Meanwhile, he had a date with a shower and a bed.

"Okay, we've got you in a room overlooking the San Jacinto Mountains. It's a lovely view and very quiet."

"Sounds great. How late does room service run?"

"Dinner until eleven and a limited menu overnight." She paused and gave him a smile of invitation. "If there's anything I can do to help you, anything at all, don't hesitate to ask."

Just what he needed, a hot fling with an employee. "Thanks for the offer," he told her, "but I think I'm all set for now."

"All right then," she said, with a hint of regret. "Enjoy your stay, sir."

"I intend to."

2

CILLA LAY ON HER STOMACH on the poolside chaise lounge and dealt the cards for yet another game of solitaire, stifling a sigh. She'd woken late, savoring the sensation of a day without appointments. Her first stop had been the spa, for a massage and facial, then a manicure and pedicure. Lying around on a chaise by the pool was the perfect way to spend the rest of the afternoon, just enjoying the sun. Relaxation, that was the theme for her weekend.

Being bored wasn't.

It made her feel inadequate. If she'd been Paige, she'd have been quite content to lie there and contemplate the universe. If she'd been Trish or Thea, books would have been company enough. But she was herself and she needed something more. Not scheduled meetings and swank party something mores, but company, conversation, fun. Solitaire wasn't cutting it.

She needed a man.

Like that gorgeous specimen who'd changed her tire, for example. If he were lying here beside her, that would be just perfect. They could laugh together, have a few drinks, do some dancing. Maybe even give each other a run through in bed, considering that here it was

April and she'd yet to have sex in the new year. Playing hard was the perfect antidote to working hard.

In retrospect, she felt silly for having been so cautious with him, especially when he'd turned out to be such a good guy. Not that she'd talked with him much, of course. In that sense, he'd been the perfect fantasy: tall, dark and handsome, a blank slate for her to color as she would. He'd be her kind of guy, the kind of guy who could make her laugh, who was just a bit unpredictable, who knew what he wanted and was ready to go after it.

Especially in bed.

Now there was a thought, much more interesting than cards. She closed her eyes, imagining how he would be. Sexy in that take charge, I've-got-to-have-you-now way. Fabulous body, that went without saying, and hands to die for. Hands that would know just how to touch her, hands that would make her shiver and moan.

Cilla sighed and opened her eyes. She wasn't quite ready to go on the prowl, even if she was on a mini-getaway, but the thought of sex—good sex—made her weak.

Oh, well. She sighed again and put the red queen on the black king. Woman on top, her favorite position.

The waitress stopped at her chaise. "Can I get anything for you?"

What the hell, Cilla thought, it was close to cocktail hour, just a couple of time zones over. She looked out toward the palm-shaded bar across the pool and considered her options. The bartender set a margarita down on the bar. Now there was an idea, something frosty and tangy tart to cut the heat. She'd have a drink and then she'd go mingle a bit and see what kind of entertainment she could scare up. "I'll have a margarita on the rocks," she began, watching the guy at the bar pick up his drink. "Ask the bartender to please use a lot of lime and add a shot of—"

Cilla broke off, eyes widening. The guy with the margarita had turned toward her enough that she saw his profile, and then his full face. What were the chances, she asked herself as the corners of her mouth began to tug up. It couldn't possibly be her Samaritan from the night before, showing up here of all places. It couldn't be.

It was.

"Scratch that order," she told the waitress. "I'll go to the bar myself."

He wore turquoise trunks, his blue-green Hawaiian shirt hanging open over them. As near as she could tell, she'd been right the night before: his body was prime stuff, washboard abs, sinewy legs, pecs that suggested he had more than a passing acquaintance with a weight room. But it was his face that captivated her.

He stared out toward the green of the golf course, nodding to the music as the breeze stirred his hair. He wore it long enough on top to be hip, short enough in the back to be tidy. The five o'clock shadow from the day before was gone, which was a pity. The gorgeous lines of cheekbone and jaw were not. Dark glasses hid his eyes.

Cilla sat up and scooped up her deck of cards. She was done with solitaire, she thought, finger-combing her hair and rising to tie on her sarong. The game she wanted to play now was deuces.

Rand stared out at the arc of mountains that rose high and sudden beyond the resort. He'd seen a lot of Europe in the past few months, but when it came to drama, the desert had it hands down.

He stifled a yawn. By dint of heroic struggle, he'd managed to stay awake the night before until about eight o'clock, then nodded off into dreams of his roadside maiden in distress, dreams in which he'd jacked up her car—and she'd jacked him up. None of which prevented him, predictably, from waking at a ridiculous hour. Even taking time to work out and linger over breakfast had still seen him on the golf course before eight. He'd practiced his driving a bit to get the rust off and then took on the full eighteen-hole course.

All things considered, he figured he'd more than made up for sitting on a plane for fourteen hours. His muscles felt pleasantly tired. Raising the margarita, he took a swallow and thought again about the woman at the side of the road. He wondered where she was, what she was doing now.

He wondered if she'd given him even a thought once he was gone.

"So how are the margaritas?"

He looked up.

It was as though his mind had conjured her up. All tropical color and silky bare skin, she stood before him, fragrant and frisky, eyes alight with the promise of fun.

And all his hormones started doing the happy dance.

Her lips curved. "The polite thing would be to invite me to sit down."

"Absolutely," he said, snapping out of it and gesturing to the stool next to him. It wasn't often that he was at a loss for words. Then again, it wasn't often just looking at a woman could make him feel sucker punched. He watched her order a drink from the bartender who had appeared immediately in that magical way they did for beautiful women. "I guess you got to where you were going."

"Thanks to you," she agreed, turning back to him. Her smile was sunbeam bright, her hair a hundred shades of blond and golden brown as it shifted with every shake of her head. She wore it chin length so that it focused attention on her face, on that full mouth, those green eyes with their mischievous tilt. A faint whisper of her scent drifted across to him. He wondered if her skin was as smooth as it looked.

"You know, if I'd guessed you were headed to the resort, I could just have given you a ride."

"Bad planning on my part."

"Don't worry about it," he said, just enjoying watching her. "I suppose if you weren't ready to get out of a car with me nearby, you probably wouldn't have gotten into one, either."

"I had your best interests at heart. What if I'd have turned out to be some wacko and there you were, stuck with me at the side of the road? You were safer with me in the car."

"You did have a tire iron," he recalled.

"Exactly."

"In that case, I guess I owe you one."

"It was the least I could do." Laughter bubbled in her voice. The bartender set down Cilla's drink and she held it up for a toast. "To good deeds and good Samaritans. Thank you again for stopping. You were very chivalrous. Your mama raised you right."

The margarita tasted tart and cool on his tongue, the tequila a faint bite underneath. "She'll be happy to hear it. You could write and tell her so. It'll make her day."

"I'll write your mother if you write mine and tell her what a cautious citizen I was," she bargained. "She's forever wailing that I'm not careful enough and I don't have the sense God gave a goat."

Rand considered her. "You look smarter than a goat."

"Thank you." She inclined her head.

"Better looking, too."

Her laugh was husky with delight. "I like to think so."

Her bikini reminded him of a dish of sherbet, all bright pink and lime-green and orange. The top of it was one of those twisted bands that seemed to stay in place magically. The whys and hows, of course, were far less interesting than what was beneath.

"So what are you doing here?" she asked, watching him.

"I was heading to Vegas and made a wrong turn at Albuquerque," he said blandly.

"What a disappointment."

"Not even remotely."

She stared at him for a beat, then blinked. "Well, just in case, I do have a deck of cards. I'll be the house and we can play a few hands," she offered.

"You're too kind."

"You can give me all your money and it'll feel just like being there."

"That would be *much* too kind."

"That's the way I am." The amusement was back.

"So what are you doing here, meeting friends?"

"Flying solo." She glanced around. "Where are your friends, Vegas?"

The palm fronds cast patterned shadows over her shoulders. Rand dragged his gaze away from her skin. "No friends."

"Not any?" She raised an eyebrow. "But you seem like such a nice person. I'll be your friend," she decided. "Didn't you tell me I owed a favor to the next person who needed one?"

"Generous of you," he said dryly.

"Isn't it just. Of course, I can afford to be generous. I'm here playing hooky from the world for a couple of days."

"Hooky works for me."

"Really?" She leaned toward him and lowered her voice like a coconspirator. "Want to play hooky together?"

"Only if you promise not to talk about anything remotely serious."

"No politics?"

"Nope."

"No economy?"

He shook his head.

"No 'So, what do you do?'"

"Absolutely not. You start down that road, I'll go find someone else's tire to change."

"Oh, now I get it," she nodded wisely, "that was your pickup move."

"You know it. I wait around the highway for gorgeous babes to have blowouts that they can't change. It's the ultimate icebreaker."

"You are smooth."

"Oh, I can ratchet up a jack with the best of 'em," he assured her.

Her eyes were bright with amusement. "I thought you looked like a man who knew his way around a lug nut."

"Just handy with tools."

She raised her glass. "Well, here's to being handy."

They grinned at each other. He'd forgotten the pleasure of banter with a clever woman, not to mention a sexy little dish like her. It had definitely been too long. "My name's Rand, by the way."

She raised an eyebrow. "Your parents wanted you to be a mapmaker?"

"Positive reinforcement," he agreed. "What's your name?"

She hesitated an instant. "Danni."

"Let me guess, your parents wanted a boy? Doesn't look like it was too successful to me."

"Au contraire. I was quite the tomboy growing up," she informed him.

He looked down to where her long, tanned legs peeked out of the wraparound sarong. "I bet you climbed trees with the best of them."

"You'd better believe it," she returned. "Played softball, too. I had a mean curveball."

"I'll remember to watch for that." He didn't know about curveballs, but she was definitely curvy enough in all the right places. "So have you been hanging out around the pool all morning?"

"Of course. Like I said, I'm playing hooky. How about you?"

"Did a quick run, played a round of golf." Didn't get down to the pool nearly soon enough.

She shook her head pityingly. "No wonder you were yawning. I'd be tired, too."

"Are you kidding? I'm just getting revved up. A dip in the water and I'll be good to go."

Invitation replaced amusement in those green eyes. "And here I thought you were pretty good already."

"Stick around. You ain't seen nothin' yet."

A JAZZ TUNE COURTESY OF A PIANIST nearby, floated out into the evening. Cilla sat in the terrace bar of the restaurant's fusion restaurant, waiting for Rand. She wasn't usually the one to wait, but when they'd parted ways to go dress for dinner, she'd found herself in a minimalist mood. Slipping into her pale gold silk shift and sandals took only a moment. The sun had taken care of her need for bronzer. All she had to do was darken her eyes a bit, slick on some lip gloss and presto, she was ready.

Staying on the grounds had seemed easiest. Neither of them had felt like dealing with the drive into Palm Springs. She couldn't quite put her finger on the point at which dinner together had become a given. As to what might happen after that, well, the long, lazy afternoon of flirting and playing like otters in the pool made that seem like a given, also.

Cilla turned her head to look at the arched entrance just as Rand came through. He stood for a moment, searching the room for her and she caught her breath.

She'd watched that face for hours at poolside, but somehow the time they'd spent apart had rendered the impact of him fresh. The afternoon sun had touched his skin with gold. Against the breezy white linen of his shirt, his hair was dark, his eyes a luminous silver. When he caught sight of her, the power of it sang through her. For a moment, he just stood, watching. Then he began to walk toward her.

And unaccountably, the breath began to clog up in her lungs.

He took his time moving across the room, as though he were savoring the spectacle. When he reached her side, he raised her fingers to his lips. "You're lovely," he said simply, brushing his lips over her knuckles.

And Cilla could only stare.

She'd been prepared for banter, for something cocky or ironic. She should have known he wouldn't be so predictable. *A man who knew what he wanted and went after it.*

"I think our table is waiting," she said.

CILLA FOLLOWED Rand off the floor in the nightclub and back to their booth, leaning back against him for a moment in mock exhaustion. Drinks to dinner, dinner to dancing. Like silent conspirators, they'd stretched the evening out, neither of them ready to see it end. With the passing hours, they moved into each other's space, as casual touches that held nothing casual within them became commonplace.

But they had yet to bridge that critical gap between possibility and certainty.

Rand's chest was hard and solid behind her and desire bubbled in her veins. When he reached out to toy with her hair, she very nearly purred. She wanted more of this man, this lovely man with the smooth voice and the bedroom eyes and the hands that promised all sorts of decadence.

She wanted more, period. So she didn't move away, only sighed when he slid an arm around her.

"You're quite a dancer," Cilla murmured.

"You inspire me."

"It's the least I can do." Then lights came up abruptly, bleaching the club from dim intimacy to hard reality. Was it really that late, she wondered in surprise, and straightened.

"Cinderella time, I guess," Rand said.

"I'm not ready to call it a night," Cilla objected. "It's too soon." Whether it was the wee hours of morning or not, she wasn't the least bit sleepy. Instead, breathless anticipation ran through her.

"You could go get your cards and we could play poker," Rand suggested.

"There's an idea. We can be like Vegas, all night, all right."

"There you go."

They walked out into the lobby of the resort, with its soaring ceilings and marble arches. Terraces ran around the edges of the atrium, the overhead lattices wound with vines to give the illusion that they were outdoors instead of in air-conditioned comfort. Rand stopped in front of a pillow-strewn brocade couch. "Go get your cards. I can wait here."

Chivalrous, perhaps, but she didn't want chivalry. She wanted much more. "How about if you just come on up, instead? That way we'll get some quiet and we've got the minibar if we get thirsty."

"From a tire iron on the highway to an invitation to your room? I think I'm making points." His voice was light, as though he wanted her to know he wasn't making any assumptions. It made her want him even more.

"You haven't lost money to me yet," she said with a grin and tugged at his sleeve. "Come on."

CILLA TOSSED DOWN a handful of dimes and nickels. "I'll see your quarter, raise you thirty cents and call." They sat on the couch in her room, cards on the upholstery between them. The French doors that led to the atrium balcony were open, bringing in the tranquil sound of falling water from the indoor fountains. A ceiling fan stirred the air, making the silk at her neckline flutter just a bit.

For the hundredth time, Rand pulled his thoughts back to the game and laid his cards down. "Eights and fives."

Cilla set down three jacks. "You are mine, baby, all mine," she crowed, and her eyes held a hot look of triumph. "That's five hands in a row."

"You never told me you were a cardsharp. Are you sure you weren't the one headed to Vegas?" If he was on a losing streak, it was because the way she'd curled those long legs underneath her, rucking up her dress just enough, played hell with his concentration. Of course, the remains of the vodka tonics on the coffee table might have a bit to do with it, as well.

And the fact that they were both wondering how and when and where they'd make the jump. Not if, though. Not if.

"A card hustler? Me? I'm just trying to give you the authentic experience," she told him, scooping up the last of his small change.

"By cleaning me out?"

"Exactly, sugar." She reached out to give his cheek a little pat. And in reflex, his hand came up to trap hers in place. Cilla froze, her eyes widening just a fraction. Surprise? Arousal? Rand curled his fingers around hers, moving them to his lips, watching her steadily. For a moment, they stared at each other, the question asked, the answer given, the knowledge of where they were going naked in their eyes.

When he released her hand, she stayed absolutely still, then she went back to shuffling the cards.

Rand looked at her in puzzlement. "What are you doing?"

"Getting ready to deal." She split the deck in two and snapped the cards together. "You're not afraid of another hand, are you?" Her eyes were bright with excitement.

"I'm out of change. You've broken me."

"Good thing you didn't make it to Vegas."

"Consider yourself lucky that I've been on a down streak. I'm usually a winner."

"Big talk," she sniffed, snapping the cards together again. "Why don't you prove it?"

"I told you, no more money."

"We could keep a tally on paper."

"That's not poker."

A smile lurked in her eyes. "You could put it on your credit card."

"I'm sure you'd love that."

Cilla spread her hands, and shrugged. "Well, the house doesn't play for free. Of course, we do have one other option."

"Yes?"

"You want stakes that mean something, I think we can arrange it." She did smile then, a slow bloom of promise.

Something deep inside him began to thud in response. "Oh yeah? What's that?"

Her eyes held a flare of recklessness. "Your clothes."

CILLA SHUFFLED the cards, excitement making her hands tremble just a bit. Rand sat shirtless, his skin gleaming gold in the light. Even though she'd seen him that afternoon in just swim trunks, he somehow seemed more naked now, his skin all the more bare for the contrast with his wheat-colored linen slacks.

They'd gone past the easy pickings. Her Manolos had been off before they'd ever started, and now Rand's Top-Siders lay nearby. Watches, jewelry, it was all on the coffee table. She'd done well the first few hands, but more recently Rand had been winning steadily.

She was beginning to run out of clothing.

Pushing the deck together, Cilla set it out for Rand to cut. When she reached out to pick up the stack, he captured her hand.

And heat zoomed up her arm.

"What are you doing?" she asked faintly.

"Just checking to see if you had any cards up your sleeve."

Her heart began to beat again. "It's a sleeveless shift."

"Can't be too careful." He ran his fingertips up the fragile skin on the inside of her forearm. Arousal whispered through her.

"Five-card draw," Cilla said, her voice a little shaky, and dealt.

Rand just watched her. He fanned his cards out and gave a small smile. It could mean he had something, it could mean he was bluffing, Cilla wasn't sure. If he had tells, she'd yet to figure them out.

Then she looked at her own hand and very nearly sighed. Three queens, a nine, and a four. She'd hold on to her ladies and take her chances with the rest, Cilla thought, tossing the other two cards down. "Two for the dealer," she said aloud. "And you, sir?"

"I'll take three."

Cilla raised an eyebrow. "Three cards for the desperate man in the corner," she said, and tossed them to him, giving herself two new cards before picking up her hand. Jubilantly, she saw that she'd drawn a pair of aces. Full house. She kept her face wooden and looked at Rand.

"I'll call," he told her.

Cilla laid down her hand. "Full house, read it and weep."

"Not quite." He put his own cards down, revealing a hand full of tens. "Four of a kind." His smile was impudent. "Looks like I win."

She cursed.

"Pretty salty language for a lady."

"That full house would have won me the last three hands."

"Timing is everything." Rand settled more comfortably on the couch, putting his hands behind his head. "Guess you should have worn a two-piece outfit."

Cilla rose. "I wore exactly the right outfit," she countered, sliding her fingers up her thighs. She heard his intake of breath as she reached the hem of her dress. Instead of pulling it up, though, she slid her hands up underneath and around to the back. The whole time she was hooking her fingers in the sides of her thong, she watched Rand. The naked hunger in his eyes made her weak. Slowly, she drew the thong down her thighs, bent over to draw it below her knees, then sat to pull it off entirely.

When she looked at him again, his chest was moving as though he'd just run up stairs. Holding the thong hooked around one finger, Cilla stretched out her arm and let the garment fall to the floor. "I believe it's your deal."

The first time Rand tried to deal, the cards slipped in his hands. He raked his hair back off his forehead and tried again.

Anticipation vaulted through her. Depending on what Rand wore beneath his linen slacks, one of them was going to be naked, more or less, when the hand was done. Certainly she would be if she lost, because she'd skipped the bra when she'd gotten dressed, thinking smugly how nice it was to be small enough that a bra was an option, not a requirement. Now, she could feel the brush of silk against her nipples.

The moment of truth, she told herself, picking up her hand to fan it out. Then she looked at the cards and swallowed. It wasn't fair, not even remotely. The previous game she'd wound up with a strong, if ultimately useless, hand. This time around?

This time, she didn't have a thing. Nothing. Nada. Not even a pair of measly twos.

Rand stared at his cards, face inscrutable, then he looked up at her.

"Discards?"

Cilla worked at breathing evenly. Maybe she could bluff. She didn't mind being naked, but she didn't want to be the first. "I'll take three," she said as casually as she could manage and hoped like hell Lady Luck would round out her hand.

Rand picked up the deck. "Nothing up my sleeves," he observed, holding open imaginary cuffs. "The lady takes a nervous three, and three for the dealer." He tossed out cards for them both as he spoke, then set the deck aside and gathered his hand.

Cilla fanned out the cards she held, then looked at them on a breath of hope.

She still had diddly. *Fold,* she telegraphed to him. *Fold, fold, fold.*

"Well, I don't see any point in betting here. Call," Rand said casually, glancing at her. Cilla felt the flush spread over her face and laid her hand down.

"Looks like I lose," she said with a calm she didn't feel.

"Or we both win, depending on how you look at it."

She rose and shook back her hair, trying to ignore the skittering in her stomach. She'd been naked with plenty of guys in her lifetime. It had never been a big deal. She knew she looked sexy, she knew they'd liked what they saw. Taking off her clothes had never bothered her before. Why now?

Because it was different to get naked with someone than it was to get naked in front of them.

Cilla turned her back to him. "Can you help me with the zipper?"

Even if she'd been unable to hear him, she'd have known he'd stepped close to her by the heat that bridged the gap between them. But she could hear the little shudder in his breath as he leaned in to her, the whisper of silk as he laid his hands on her hips. His breath tickled the fine hairs on her skin. Then she felt the brush of his lips on the nape of her neck and she gave a little helpless sound.

Warm, soft, the touch of his lips made her shiver, made her stiffen.

Made her want.

Desire began to drum through her. She needed to taste him, she needed the feel of his mouth on hers. Weak with anticipation, Cilla let her head drop back. And oh, God, all the waiting was worth it. Pleasure bloomed as he pressed his mouth to hers. For an instant it was as though every nerve in her body was concentrated in her lips, the sensations overwhelming everything else.

Or not quite everything else, because she could feel his hands moving up her sides, tracing the dip in her waist, the line of her ribs. The featherlight strokes gave promise of what was to come when he was touching her, instead. He broke the kiss.

And she waited.

When his hands rose to her zipper, he drew it down slowly, touching only the fabric, not her. Cilla shuddered as the cool air touched the narrow stripe of exposed flesh. She knew when he'd dropped it low enough to realize that she had no bra on; she heard his helpless exhalation.

And with a sound of impatience she turned to him.

3

His HANDS SLID the dress off her shoulders. Cilla gave
an absent shrug, releasing the fabric to pool around her
feet even as she reached out for his waistband. After a
day of temptation, a night of promise, here in the wee,
wee hours it was finally happening. She unfastened his
trousers and let them drop away.

When she stepped forward to press her body
against his, the heat and hard muscle and smooth skin
nearly made her swoon. Pleasure saturated her, the
feel of his hands running down her back, molding her
to him, the insistent pressure of his hard cock against
her belly. She wanted him on her and in her, she
wanted him—

Cilla broke their kiss and pressed her head to his
chest with a groan.

"What?"

"Do you happen to have any condoms with you?"
she asked, a little desperately.

His hands froze. "Shit."

"Exactly."

After a moment, he began exploring her again. "It's
not the end of the earth, you know," he murmured, running a line of kisses over her shoulder as he slid one

hand up to her breast. "There are other things we can do. We have the technology."

Cilla laughed. "I suppose you're right."

"Not that I'm not flattered that you think so highly of my hard-on."

Cilla looked down to see it bobbing and jerking. "Looks like it thinks highly of me, too."

RAND HAD SPENT the better part of the card game trying to ignore the tight coil of tension in his belly, trying to ignore the brush of skin and fabric as his cock lengthened under his clothes. Now, the pressure of her fingers, the motion of the thin skin over the hard column of flesh had his breath hissing in. It was too soon. He wanted to savor the feel of her taut, sleek body, listen to her pleasure, and then, only then, find his own release.

He reached down and stilled her hand, then pulled her to him. She tasted just as she sounded, tangy and sweet, with a complexity that made him linger over her mouth even as he sought his own pleasure by finding her breast. The slight curve of it against his palm gave him a pulse of arousal. He squeezed the hard nipple until she moaned.

And the sound only made him harder. Rand reached for the lamp.

She caught at his hand. "What are you doing?"

"I figured you'd want the lights off."

"Why?"

"The women I've been with like it dark."

Cilla smiled wickedly. "I'd say you've been hanging around with the wrong crowd," she said, drawing him to the bed.

"Doors open?" This time, surprise crept into his voice.

Cilla laughed and fell back against the mattress. "If they're up at 3:00 a.m. and have sharp enough eyes to see all the way up here, more power to them."

In fact, she thought, it was a bit of a turn-on to think about someone watching them together, watching him kneel by the bedside and part her knees so that he could lick his way up her thighs. How was it that she registered the warm, tempting touch inches away from where it was actually happening, inches away in that hidden cleft where she was already slick with wanting?

The first contact was just a tease, a quick brush of soft heat that made her jolt and left her craving more. The second lasted longer, sliding through her sensitive folds to find her for an instant. By then, though, his hands were on her breasts, rubbing the nipples to send quicksilver bolts of wanting through her. She pressed her body against him, needing his touch, needing more, needing it all.

And suddenly his mouth was on her, tearing a shocked cry from her throat.

Cilla's fingers clutched at the coverlet, then Rand's shoulders as her hips moved against him. He wouldn't be rushed, though. He took her close but backed away, leaving her wanting before taking her up again, driving her mindless. Spiraling tension gripped her, making her a slave to the wet heat of his tongue until he gave her that crucial extra second and the good, hard orgasm broke through her.

She didn't know how long it lasted, the helpless quaking, the incoherent cries, the washes of pleasure that came at her again and again. She couldn't say how long it took her to recover enough to talk. Finally, she lay still, aftershocks still jolting her body at intervals.

Rand rose to lay on the bed beside her, propping his head up on his hand.

"You know, I kind of like this strip poker," he said, running the flat of his hand over her belly.

"Give me a minute." Cilla's voice was ragged. "You'll like it even more once I can move."

"I've got time."

The sound of the fountains in the atrium drifted in through the open French doors. Time was irrelevant. Eventually, Cilla rose to press him flat on his back.

Rand's cock was still hard. He could feel the throb of the blood rushing through it. Anticipation, he thought. It was almost as good as the reality of sex, the expectation bubbling in his blood, the nerve endings sensitized so that even the drift of air stirred by the ceiling fan had his erection twitching against his belly. And then he felt the warmth of her breath, the nuzzle of her lips. A sigh escaped him.

She didn't tease, though, seeming to understand how close he already was. Instead, the electric heat of her tongue stroked up the underside of his cock and pure lust slammed through him. When she slid him into the warm wetness of her mouth, he groaned. He fought desperately to stay in the moment, to not let the rhythmic strokes take him past the point of inevitability.

He wanted to prolong it, and when he went, he wanted to take her with him.

"Why don't you swing around here so that we can both enjoy ourselves," he managed to say, grinding his teeth as she stopped her ministrations.

"You mean…"

He reached down to help her move into place, running his hands along her long, lovely thighs as she slid his cock back into her mouth.

How much sensation could one person absorb, Cilla wondered as she felt Rand's tongue trace maddening patterns over her clit even as she savored his erection. The next best thing to having it inside her was the immediacy of having it against her lips, of hearing his groan when she changed her motion, added her hand. But even as she brought him closer to coming, he was doing the same for her, each slippery stroke making the heat and tension rise within her, sometimes making her stop just to moan out her pleasure. In between, she savored him, drawing him closer and closer to that point at which the world ceased to be about anything but sensation.

And then it wasn't anything but sensation, her own surging pleasure and the shuddering soon after in his body as he released and let himself follow.

IT WAS THE SOUNDS from the atrium, coming in through the open French doors, that woke her the first time. Cilla crossed over to close the doors and shut the blinds against the pitiless day.

"What time is it?" Rand rasped.

She squinted at the digital clock. "Nine." Only three hours after they'd finally gone to sleep. It was easy to slide back into oblivion.

When she woke again, it was closer to one, and real life was beginning to gather at the edges of her mind. The Danforth cocktail reception was less than five hours away and she needed to get her game face on. Board members, managers, lawyers…she might know them all, but that didn't mean she didn't have to make a good impression.

Showing up looking freshly boffed was probably out of the question.

The hot water in the shower beating on her cleared her mind and left her with that wonderful sense of well-being that followed a night of truly great sex. Or a few hours of it, anyway. She'd found herself a clever, talented lover, indeed, she thought, smiling at herself in the mirror as she dried off.

Cilla wrapped herself in a towel and walked into the room to find the blinds open and Rand sitting out on the balcony in just his pants, the newspaper open on his lap.

He smiled at her. "Good morning."

She spent a moment or two just staring at him. Such a beautiful, beautiful man. "Good morning."

"You do nice things for a towel," he said, and rose to cross to her.

Cilla lost long minutes to his kiss, and then the feel of his hands when the towel dropped. It would be so easy to slide back into bed and let him take her away.

Easy but not smart. She took a deep breath and moved back from him, plucking her towel from the floor. "As much as I would love to dive back in with you, my hooky's over. Time to go back to the real world."

Disappointment flickered over his face. "I was hoping for a rematch."

"No can do. Sorry."

He sighed. "I suppose you're right."

"Being a grown-up sucks." Every fiber hummed and waited as she hoped to hear some word of the future. For God's sake, they hadn't even properly had sex. They couldn't let it drop here. Edgy with nerves, she crossed to the closet and pulled out some underwear.

Rand grabbed his shirt from the floor and put it on. "So where do you live?"

She slid into a denim miniskirt and a Mark Jacobs T-shirt. "L.A. And you?"

"I travel a lot, but L.A. is sort of my base." He buttoned his shirt and turned to her. "Can I call you next time I'm in town?"

She beamed—she couldn't help it. "I'd like that."

He scooped her against him. "I'd like that, too."

THE USUAL FACES, Cilla thought that evening, as she walked into the Danforth cocktail reception. The usual conversations. Danforth had reserved a private atrium room at the resort for the welcome dinner. Standing in little groups by the floor-to-ceiling windows were the five board members, most of the division heads for Forth's, the department managers for Danforth and the financial cadre. It was maybe fifteen or sixteen people all told, the brain trust of the Danforth empire.

Given that she wasn't in the direct management chain, she probably ought to have been pleased to be involved.

She wasn't.

What she was was frustrated that she'd had to work twice as hard and twice as long as any normal employee to make headway in the company. Only when she'd sent in her résumé under a false name and received an immediate callback on a management position had she been able to get her father to take her seriously.

He'd spent much of his lifetime dismissing his wife.

He wasn't going to dismiss Cilla.

She watched him now as he stood by the windows talking with the CFO, the head of legal and a board member. Sam Danforth wasn't particularly tall, but something about the way he held himself commanded attention. She could see herself in the cleft of his chin and the green of his eyes, the eyes she often felt didn't really see the grown-up her. And until he saw her and respected her, no one in his chain of command was really going to do so.

She could tolerate that for the time being. Cilla was nothing if not patient. She'd gotten the education, she'd gotten the experience. She'd grown up learning strategy from her father. Now all she needed was the opportunity to prove what she could do.

With the skill of long practice, she stepped into the room and began circulating, a chat here, a joke there. Having a drink to hold on to kept her hands busy, though she'd learned from her father long ago to stick with club soda and lime at business receptions. "You've got to keep your wits about you," he maintained. "You never know what might come up and you want that edge."

Her father turned now and waved her over. She'd known the men he was talking with since she'd been in braces.

"Here she is, our secret weapon," her father said.

"How go the fashion wars?" asked Danforth's CFO Bernard Fox, portly but still dapper in a beautifully cut Armani suit.

"A Hun dressed in Versace is still a Hun," Cilla said lightly.

"Good point. I hear Sam here wants us to come up with a strategy for thirty percent growth over the next three years," said Burt Ruxton, longtime board member. "Since you're the first timer at the meeting, we'll let you come up with it."

"Are you still holding a grudge over that time I dropped your satellite phone in the swimming pool, Uncle Burt?"

"Not at all. Although if profits go up thirty percent, you might finally get around to replacing it."

Cilla's father looked over her shoulder and brightened. "Ah. Here's someone I want you to meet. About time you showed up," he said more loudly.

"Checking my e-mail," said a voice behind her.

A very familiar voice.

And Cilla turned and found herself nose to nose with Rand Mitchell.

"Rand, this is my daughter, Cilla. Cilla, this is Rand Mitchell. He's doing some business development for us in Europe."

She'd always thought jaws dropping was a figure of speech, at least until her own did. Surprise? Shock, more accurately. And she couldn't help it. She laughed.

A corner of Rand's mouth tugged up into a rueful smile in response.

"What's the joke?" her father demanded, looking between them. "Do you two know each other?"

"Sort of," she managed, working to tuck away her amusement. "I had a flat on the highway coming in and Rand was my good Samaritan." He stood now in a gorgeous suit, looking polished, professional and entirely good enough to eat.

That probably wasn't such a good idea anymore, she thought. Getting her body to agree, of course, was going to be the challenge.

"Well." Sam Danforth clapped Rand on the shoulder. "Nice to see that you're looking after Danforth's important assets. Rand is our man in Europe," he said to the rest of the group and introduced Rand around. "Thanks to him, we're finally making a name for ourselves over there."

"I bet you're making a name here, too," Cilla said.

SOMEONE, SOMEWHERE, Rand was fairly sure, had written a "Top Ten Business Don'ts" list, and at the top of that list had to be sleeping with the boss's daughter. Stupid, brainless, dense. Normally, he'd be kicking himself up one side of the room and down the other.

Oddly, he wasn't. The whole thing was too absurd to be taken seriously. After all, what were the chances?

As a committed fast-tracker, he supposed he had to wonder what impact his adventure with Danni—or Cilla, it now appeared—might have on his future. Then again, he'd never planned to stay at Danforth longer than the obligatory year, maybe less, if something appealing came calling.

"So you're our man in Milan," said Cilla.

"Cilla's the couture buyer for Danforth's and does some of the bridge-line buying for Forth's," her father put in. "We'll have to get her involved with the European branches. Maybe you two can find some time to hunker down over that while we're here."

"We'll be sure to do that," Rand said blandly, wondering just what Papa Danforth would say about the kind of hunkering they'd been doing already.

Cilla kept a poker face. Of course, it didn't do to think about poker at this point. Or getting her naked and having his hands on all that warm skin, or the way her body shuddered when he—

"So you're the dot-com whiz." Ruxton eyed him speculatively.

If "whiz" defined a man who'd made the better part of three million in an IPO and pissed three quarters of it away in a venture capital firm, maybe. Instead of raking in the bucks from the bonanza of IPOs launched by the legions of bright young things he'd funded, Rand had watched his investments die or go into hibernation, waiting for the market to return before considering an IPO. Until they went public, he couldn't get his money back. Maybe one day, but it wouldn't be any time soon.

Rand smiled briefly. "It was a wild ride while it lasted."

Cilla tilted her head at him. "Would you do it again?"

He considered her question, well aware that his audience was far bigger than just her. "The experience didn't make me afraid of taking chances—I think your biggest returns always come from thinking outside the box, and risk is always part of that. I learned a lot about moderation and hedging my bets, though. I'm probably better at gauging a situation than I was," he added.

A response suitable for a job interview, Rand thought in satisfaction, which, in a way, this was. He'd spent the four months since he'd come on board at Danforth getting the Milan venture rolling. No one knew him, aside from looking at the reports on his project. Never hurt to impress the board, he figured.

Granted, the Danforth job didn't represent the degree of challenge he was accustomed to, and the company was sure as hell a lot more conservative. Then again, by the time they'd come calling, he'd been unemployed for a year, waiting for the right opportunity to arise. A year, at his level, you could justify; more than that made you look like a problem candidate to future employers. So even though he hadn't needed the money he'd said yes, reasoning that the European expansion was marginally interesting to him. Besides, any job that entailed being in stores that dressed beautiful women couldn't be all bad.

"So you're comfortable being back in the bricks-and-mortar world?" Fox watched him closely.

"If I weren't, I wouldn't be here," Rand said with perfect truth. He wasn't one of those idealists who thought everything about the world was going to go Internet, he was just a businessman who'd recognized potential when he saw it.

The cocktail hour wore on and he shook hands and made appropriately incisive or off-the-cuff remarks, depending on how he judged the situation. Out of the corner of his eye, he saw Cilla head out of the room.

He circulated long enough to be discreet, then followed.

The foyer was lit with the warm light of sunset reflecting in through the wall of windows. Cilla stood near them, Mt. San Jacinto providing her backdrop.

"Danni? As in Danforth?"

"It was the best I could come up with." She turned and looked at him apologetically. "It's like Paris Hilton, people recognize the name, and I didn't want to be recognized."

"We swapped numbers this morning." And it left him feeling shut out.

"I would have said something once I knew you better," she told him. "It's just hard. There are the stores and there's all this money and I just wanted this morning to be about us…" She trailed off. "Does that make sense?"

Slowly, he nodded. He might not like it, but he could understand it. "So it never occurred to you that the guy you met in the hotel bar could be here for the Danforth meeting?"

"Did it occur to you in my case?" she countered.

He shrugged. "I knew Danforth had a daughter, but I thought you stayed out of management," he told her.

"And I thought I knew all of our people who were going to be here. Sergio Venetti is running the Milan store. I've met him."

"I don't run the stores. I'm business development. All I do is set things up, buy the property, get construction started. Then I turn it over to someone else."

"That explains a lot," she said, nodding.

"Anyway, I was a late addition here," he admitted. "Command performance from the boss."

"Well, when God calls…"

"Exactly." He studied her, feeling a little surge of frustration at the fact that she was now off-limits. She wore one of the prim and pretty suits that had been the spring runway rage. Somehow seeing her ladylike and demure clothes just gave him more of an urge to get them off her and uncover the uninhibited lover he'd discovered the night before. "Is this going to be a problem, us working together?" It was definitely going to be for him, unless he got a grip on his imagination.

"Gee, I think it might be, considering the fact that we work in different departments, on separate continents." Her voice was dry. She grinned at him. "Relax, it'll be fine. This time next week, you'll be back in Milan."

"London," he corrected.

"Wherever. I think we're both smart enough to keep a handle on it. No harm, no foul."

That was overstating the case. It had certainly done harm to him—to his peace of mind, anyway. And yet, as much as he knew how narrowly they'd avoided trouble, he was glad they hadn't figured out what was going on until after the fact, because the fact had been pretty damned memorable.

Cilla put out her hand. "We cool?"

"We cool." He shook with her, letting go as quickly as he could. Before he really registered the feel of her skin.

Cilla blew out a breath. "Oh-kay. I'm going to hit the ladies' room. That way we won't walk back in together."

"Worried about your father suspecting something?"

"I'm not, no," she said frankly. "But it might be best for you if we keep our distance."

He knew she was a creature of warmth, of humor, of appetites. Now, here was something he hadn't expected—her concern.

Color stained her cheeks at his pleased stare. "What?"

Rand couldn't prevent the smile. "Taking care of me?"

"Oh, well, just…paying back the good deed."

He itched to brush his lips over hers. Off-limits, he reminded himself. "You've got a nice soft side, Priscilla," he murmured.

"Only my grandmother ever called me that," she muttered uncomfortably.

"You've got a nice soft side," he repeated. "I'm glad I could be your Samaritan."

4

MORNING CAME far too quickly for Cilla's taste. Her father was of the lark persuasion and assumed everyone else was happy starting at seven-thirty. Of course, as president, CEO and chief shareholder of Danforth, she supposed he was entitled to think whatever he liked. What she thought, as she found a seat, was that nine o'clock would have been far more popular.

The conference room was furnished in dark wood and jewel-toned linens. No spectacular views here. The focus now was on work. The Danforth groups sat around an open rectangle of tables, a briefing book before each person. Pitchers of water and dishes of candy sat at intervals on the dark green table coverings. To one side, a breakfast buffet groaned with eggs and bacon and fruit, but at this hour Cilla couldn't even think about it. All she wanted was coffee and consciousness.

Luckily, nothing on the early-morning agenda required any preparation from her, so she was able to merely absorb caffeine until she was marginally awake. Then Rand walked in and sat next to her. Butterflies fluttered around in her stomach even as she gave him a professional smile and nod. No way was she going to risk shaking hands.

She turned to the manager on her other side, chatting casually until her father brought the meeting to order. That should do it, she thought as the various department heads began reporting on the new business ventures, submitting to merciless grillings by her father and the board. Cilla didn't bother to open her briefing book. She'd studied all the material ahead of time. Be prepared was one of her father's mottos, and she'd taken it very much to heart.

It was interesting to watch Rand as he found himself on the hot seat, summarizing his work on the Milan store and the European expansion in general. Danforth had sunk a fair chunk of change into the venture, and the responsibility sat squarely on Rand's shoulders. Still, he seemed to be at ease, even enjoying himself. Of course, through a combination of luck and skill, his news was rosy, which always simplified things.

His suit today was camel colored with a white shirt and a tie of pale gold patterned with gray. "We're planning the grand opening of the Milan store in two weeks." Rand looked around the room, focusing on her father. "The returns from the first month are strong. I think we've got a winner."

"What comes next?" The present never counted so much to her father as the future. Being two steps ahead was the only way to compete.

"I'm in negotiations on properties in London and Zurich, and investigating Berlin."

"Why not Paris?" her father demanded. "That was the initial plan."

It didn't faze Rand. "After my preliminary investigations, I reconsidered, as I reported in my February 5 memo. I think we should take the easy pickings first. Paris is a very competitive market. Let's get the other properties rolling. We can perfect our marketing and stock for the European clientele, build buzz so that we've got more bounce when we go into Paris."

Smooth, Cilla thought, very smooth. There were nods and mutterings of agreement from around the room, and they moved on.

"One last item to cover in business development," her father announced. "Our boutique venture on Melrose Avenue, Danforth Annex."

And Sam Danforth didn't look happy about it. "Let's dispense with this one quickly and move on to strategic planning. As most of you know, Stewart Law put this one together, he has since resigned."

Poor Stewart, Cilla thought sympathetically. She might not have agreed with his execution, but there was no doubt he'd put everything he had into making the store work.

"If you'll look in your briefing books," her father continued, "you'll see the financials for the first year of operation."

Paper rustled as people turned to the appropriate page. Someone whistled. Cilla didn't even bother to look. She knew the numbers by heart.

"Off plan is one thing. This is a complete failure," Danforth pronounced. "Unfortunately, it's still our problem. The question is, what do we do?"

Cilla felt the hairs rise on the back of her neck. This was it. This was the opportunity she'd been waiting for. She'd done her research. As soon as she saw the opening, she was going to dive for it.

"You going to bring in a tiger team?" one of the board members asked.

Danforth shook his head. "I don't see the point. The concept doesn't work. I plan to close it and cut our losses. The market in L.A. clearly won't support more than one Danforth store."

Close down a property on Melrose? Cilla stared at her father. It was sheer lunacy. "If you give up the space, you'll be compounding one strategic error with another," she heard herself saying calmly.

Around the room, heads turned, first to her, then to her father. Danforth wasn't at the head of the table—with the arrangement, there wasn't any such thing—but he was the one everybody looked to, even so. And by his reaction, he wasn't amused. "I'm looking at a strategic error of about seven million dollars. How is breaking a lease going to compound that?"

"Giving up an opportunity to make money is just as bad as losing capital, and if you walk away from Danforth Annex, that's just what you'll be doing."

"We don't just need a modest sales increase at this store," he said impatiently. "It has to completely reverse, and I don't see a way to do that. We need to recognize that the Danforth concept is not working there and go on."

"Exactly." It was just the opening she needed. "The Danforth concept hasn't worked there because the people who come to Melrose are not the same people who shop at the Rodeo Drive store."

"If we're not looking at a clientele with the money to support the boutique, then we should pull out," Bernard Fox put in.

Cilla shook her head. "It's not a question of money. The people who shop upper Melrose have plenty of it, but they're not looking for their mother's store. Even if they like the clothes, they'll go elsewhere. Danforth appeals to a certain—" she searched for a diplomatic term "—conservatively stylish client. They want beautiful clothing, but nothing too edgy, and they want to buy it in a quiet, luxurious environment. That won't work for Danforth Annex."

"And I suppose you're going to tell me what will work?" Her father's voice was dry.

Cilla grinned. "Of course. I'm your target demographic. I want a store with some energy, some fun. I want clothes that break the rules, clothes that aren't for sedate lunches but for clubs, concerts, premieres."

"What kind of a product line do you see Danforth Annex carrying?" asked Ruxton.

"A similar price range, but from edgier designers like Gaultier, Versace, the ones creating controversy. We also want the new designers who are just getting the buzz going. They won't all sell immediately, but they'll add to the draw of the store." Her voice vibrated with enthusiasm. Oh, she knew just how it should go, and for once she was getting a chance to say so. "We'll be the place for people to come to, to buy the cutting edge. The sexiest, the barest outfits that stars will wear to annual shows and parties so that word will get around."

"It looks like we've already dumped a considerable sum into marketing," Ruxton observed. "Even if we did revamp the store, we'd be hard-pressed to counteract the current impression. Rebranding takes an enormous amount of money."

"Word of mouth will help, as a start. I can work my media contacts. Maybe we persuade a couple of the smaller designers to hold shows in the store." Cilla paused. It wasn't smart, but the temptation was too strong for her to resist. "There is one other angle that could really work for us." She hesitated, then hurried on. "I've been working on a lingerie line, Cilla D. Very provocative and very luxurious. That ought to get us footage in all the magazines and the *Times*. Think of it, Danforth Annex as the launch of the Danforth heiress's line."

"We are not going to fund a vanity project for you," Danforth thundered.

"It's not a vanity project," she flared, then modulated her voice. "It's a publicity angle. I'm trying to tell you ways to make this work."

"Whatever it is, it's not appropriate." His face got that closed expression that told her he'd stopped listening. "Danforth Annex was an attempt to broaden the Danforth brand. What you're talking about is not the Danforth brand."

"Sure it is," said Rand, next to her. "Just as Forth's is the Danforth brand downscaled for the mainstream. You want to catch your Danforth customer of twenty years from now, you hook them with Danforth Annex. Sooner or later, they'll walk through the door and realize they're too old for it, but by then you've got them. That's when they start looking to the flagship store."

Bernard Fox considered. "Do you think she's right about the stock?"

"I wouldn't push it as far as she's proposing," Rand answered, "but I agree that you've got a different clientele there that you've got to address if you want to succeed. We could carry over the elements of Danforth that work and bring in some fresh air to complement them." He leaned back and propped one elbow on the back of his chair. "It's the same approach we've taken in a different way with Danforth Milan, and that we'll take for Danforth London. You've got to tailor the store to the customer, not expect the customer to follow the store."

"Danforth has got to move into the twenty-first century or it's not going to survive," Cilla said passionately. "We've got to take chances. Isn't that what you've always said?" she appealed to her father.

"We've already lost millions based on a chance we took. We can't afford to repeat that."

"We won't," she shot back. "I've done an analysis. I can make this work, I'm sure of it." She was getting too emotional again, she knew it. With effort, she toned her voice down. "Look, you're ready to shut it down. Why not try something different? I know the clientele, I know the market. Give me a chance. I can turn it around, I swear." How had it turned from a business discussion to her once again pleading to be taken seriously, to be given a fraction of the respect accorded to Rand, for example?

Sam Danforth looked at his watch. "I think it's time we took a break," he said wearily. "Cilla, the board and I will discuss this and have an answer for you when we reconvene. Fifteen minutes, people."

And that, she thought dejectedly, was very likely the end of that.

"NICE PITCH IN THERE," Rand murmured.

They stood out in the foyer with the rest of the non-board members, waiting for the doors to open. "For all the good it did," Cilla said, hearing the whisper of bitterness in her words.

"You don't know that," he pointed out. "We're going on half an hour, here, and they're still in closed session. You should consider that a good sign."

"What is my father thinking, talking about pulling out of Melrose Avenue?"

Rand smiled. "Scandalous."

"Foolish," she countered. "It's a bad business decision. I don't like seeing us make mistakes." Why wouldn't they listen to her, and why wouldn't they give her a chance? "I wish—"

"What?"

There was something about those eyes, something she could get lost in. It wasn't about sex now, it was about needing a friend. "Just once I wish he'd listen to me. He never takes what I say seriously, and because he doesn't, the board doesn't, either." The familiar frustration welled up.

"Maybe it's the way you say it." Rand's voice was mild.

She bristled. "Meaning I should sugarcoat it? Why should I have to? You can say what's on your mind and people accept it. Why can't I?"

"You can say whatever you like, but not if you're looking to get what you want. To do that, you have to present things differently, same way I did with the Paris thing." He shrugged. "They're in business to make money. Show them the value proposition and they'll listen."

"I thought that was what I was doing."

"But you brought your emotions into it. You made it personal, and when it's personal, they can walk away. That's the thing to remember, it's not personal, it's business."

She looked at him, standing there in his beautiful suit, and sighed. "That's what I want it to be, but it always winds up being personal for me because ultimately I'm still his daughter, and that's how he treats me."

"Maybe he's having a hard time accepting that his little girl has grown up. Show him you have. Act like you would if you were reporting to someone who doesn't know you from Adam. Show them how giving you what you want gets them what they want."

"I did that."

Rand grinned. "Sort of, but your agenda came through loud and clear. Try ratcheting it back some next time around."

He was right, she thought with a sinking heart. After all of her planning and research, she'd let her emotions run away with her. "I hate finding out that I've been an idiot," she muttered.

"I think that's too strong a word. You gave them something to chew on, you just need to polish your presentation a little. It'll come, trust me."

The reassurance, the kind words helped. It was good advice. The next time she'd nail it. "Thanks for the voice of support in there. You seemed like the only one who got what I was talking about."

"Don't mistake me, I don't entirely agree with what you're proposing, at least not for a company like Danforth," he warned her. "I think some of what you said is sound, though. It was the right idea, and with a little adjustment you could—" He broke off at the sight of the meeting-room doors opening.

"Why do I feel like we should be looking for black smoke or white smoke," Cilla said under her breath. Burt Ruxton winked at her as she walked in and sat down.

Her father surveyed the room as everyone took their seats. "Well, you gave us some things to think about with the Annex, Cilla, obviously. We weren't able to come to any initial agreement beyond the fact that we shouldn't pull out of the Melrose store without taking another run at it."

Clearly, he wasn't entirely in agreement with the decision. For all that Sam Danforth was the majority stockholder, though, the board held the other forty percent of the company and they had a voice in strategic moves like this one. And maybe they'd hand her the opportunity. She felt a little surge of excitement.

"There's been some debate about how, exactly, to move forward." And it fried him, Cilla could see. Still, he'd needed the influx of capital back when he'd gone looking for Danforth investors, and he had to live with the situation he'd created.

Even if it meant finally giving his daughter the authority she'd earned.

"Clearly, what we've got isn't working. The question is how conservative the new model needs to be. But that's yours to figure out," he said briskly, glancing at her and then looking around the room. Effervescence began to fizz in Cilla's veins. "We've decided to fund the Annex for another six months. It's going to need to meet some pretty strict milestones," he stipulated, "but we're going to give the two of you a chance with it."

The two of them?

"Can you back up a minute?" Cilla fought to keep her voice calm, staring at her father. "What two of us?" It had been her idea. They couldn't give it to someone else.

"Rand weighed in with a scenario, too," he pointed out.

"The vote was split between the two directions," Ruxton explained. "Part of the problem is that, well, to be frank, you've never run a project before, Cilla. You're a buyer."

Because she'd never had a chance for anything more, she wanted to rant. She'd run projects when she'd been earning her M.B.A. She just needed to be given a chance. "Rand's a business development person. He doesn't run stores, either."

"Rand's got project management experience, you know retail. It's up to you to find a way to work it," Ruxton added placatingly. "We couldn't come to a conclusive decision on direction, so we thought it was best to put the project to the two of you as a team." The worst part was that Uncle Burt thought he'd managed to do something good for her, she thought. He didn't understand that it was like saddling her with a baby-sitter.

"It's an understandable decision, but there's one big problem," Rand said calmly. "I'm up to my elbows in work on the London and Zurich stores. I won't be able to get over here often and I don't know how much use I'll be able to be long-distance."

"We've taken care of that. We'll pass your European projects off to Ken." Her father pointed to the business development manager for Forth's. "You've done enough of the groundwork that he should be able to pick it up."

She was close enough to Rand to see his jaw tighten, though she doubted anyone else noticed. "These kinds of projects are about relationships." His voice was even. "We're at a very delicate point in the negotiations. Switching the contact person now could break the deal and cost us money."

"Then make sure that doesn't happen," her father said in a tone that brooked no argument. "This is a temporary assignment but an important one. I want you to make sure it's done right."

Let Rand see what it felt like to be steamrollered by Sam Danforth, Cilla thought grimly. So much for reasonable advice.

Her father, meanwhile, remained oblivious. "Rand, you and Ken should plan to spend a couple of hours this week mapping out a basic timeline. I'd like to see you in L.A. ready to work on Danforth Annex no later than two weeks from now. Sit down with Cilla before you go, as well. After all, you two are going to be partners."

5

RAND WALKED UP to the wall of windows and stared out at the city of Los Angeles spread out seventeen stories below.

"The Wilshire Corridor is a very prestigious address," said the real estate woman from behind him. Ellen? No, Eleanor. "It's quite the neighborhood for up-and-coming professionals. You're lucky to find a corner unit like this." Her heels tapped briskly on marble tile as she led him back through the kitchen area. "The owner, Ian Cresswell, is spending a year on assignment in Australia."

"Do I have to take it for the whole year?" Rand walked past the kitchen to the bedrooms.

"No, of course not. We could do it on a revolving six-month lease, with sixty days' notice of vacating."

The views he liked, and high ceilings and walls of windows made the space airy and open. The furnishings, though? Ian Cresswell had seen a few too many swinging bachelor movies, it appeared. "Does the furniture stay?"

"This is a very chic look, Mr. Mitchell. Very Italian. Very of the moment."

Or very not. Given that he'd just come from Italy,

he was in a perfect position to call her on it, but it wasn't worth bothering over. The project was going to last for six months. Not long enough to pull his own stuff out of storage, at least not most of it. Maybe some of his music, some of his small collection of art. For six months, he could ignore the black leather and chrome and soak up the view.

Still, he thought longingly of his town home in Boston, currently leased and off-limits to him. Even the apartment in Milan had been better. During his months in Italy, he'd picked up a nice piece of furniture here and there, and the place had been coming together. Rand stifled a sigh. The Italian furniture would go into storage with the rest of his belongings. At some point, he'd settle down enough to bring it all out again. While his life was in flux, though, it would have to stay out of sight.

All he needed now was a temporary roosting place.

He looked at her. "When can I move in?"

"ALL YOU PEOPLE getting all mushy," Delaney complained, looking from Kelly to Sabrina to Trish. They sat clustered around tables, amid the detritus of dinner. "We're going to have to kick you out of the Supper Club and start restricting it to us single chicks."

"I'm still single," Kelly objected.

"You're cohabiting." Delaney dismissed her. "It's practically the same thing as being married."

"What about me?" Trish piped up. "I'm not doing either."

"Say the words 'Ty Ramsay,'" Delaney ordered.

Trish's look turned dreamy. "Ty Ramsay," she repeated obediently, her lips tugging up into a smile.

Delaney shook her head sadly. "It's just a matter of time."

Trish fairly glowed, and had ever since she'd gotten involved with Sabrina's cousin the previous fall, Cilla thought fondly. Though she still dressed casually, there was a flash and a friskiness that hadn't been there before. She'd changed, and Ty had been a part of that. It really was just a matter of time.

"So, I rest my case," Delaney announced. "You should all be banished to the far end of the table if you're not going to contribute."

"Well, it's not like you've been exactly regaling us with stories," Paige told her.

Delaney crossed her legs, flipping her short, flowered skirt. "I'm taking the week off."

"What about the tortured artist?" Thea asked. "I thought he was your hunka hunka burning love."

"Intense men take so much energy," Delaney sighed. "He wore me out. Plus, he wanted to paint me, which was sexy at first, especially the first few times we got playing with the paint," she added thoughtfully. "After a while, though…do you have any idea how long you have to pose for a painting?" she demanded.

"So what we're really talking about here is your limited attention span," Thea said.

"It's someone else's turn to come up with a story," Delaney told her. "What about you."

"I've had my fill of guys for a few years, thanks," Thea responded. As usual, her hair was skinned back from her face and she wore completely unflattering black glasses. Cilla wondered, not for the first time, why Thea changed after college, what had happened to her while she'd been a model in New York? She wasn't like Trish, who'd merely ignored her appearance. Thea seemed to actively work on ways to disguise herself.

"Oh, come on, Thea, I bet we could set you up with our waiter," Delaney said, tempting.

Thea looked down. Cilla figured it couldn't hurt to run some interference for her. "Forget that," she announced. "Let me tell you about my week."

"So HERE I'M THINKING I'm going to get this great chance to prove myself and instead I get saddled with a watchdog," Cilla finished, fuming anew at the situation.

There was a short silence at the table while they digested her story. "I don't know, it seems to me like you ought to be excited," Thea said, twirling her wineglass on the table.

"The board pushed your father into giving you an opportunity," Trish agreed.

"With a baby-sitter who's not going to let me do a single thing they wouldn't approve of." Even Cilla could hear the sour note in her voice.

Paige considered. "That's kind of their job, isn't it?"

"That doesn't mean I have to like it."

"Is this a 'poor baby' moment?" Sabrina asked sympathetically, laughter in her eyes.

Cilla pushed out her lower lip. "Yes."

"Oh, poor baby," they all said in a chorus, the ones nearest patting her.

"Thank you," Cilla said with dignity.

"So enough of the 'poor babys,' what's the guy like?" Delaney wanted to know.

Cilla sighed. "Gorgeous."

"Tell," she demanded.

"Cheekbones you could cut titanium with. Dark hair that kind of falls over his forehead. Great body, fabulous shoulders." Remembering the way they'd felt under her fingers had her drifting off for a moment.

Delaney gave her an amused look. "You could tell the shoulders part through a business suit?"

"Not exactly."

Paige raised a manicured eyebrow. "How not exactly?"

"Well, we, um, sort of slept together."

"What?" The level of synchronization was impressive, Cilla thought, considering it came out of six throats simultaneously.

"You're taking charge of the situation right away, I see," Delaney said in admiration. "Get 'em by the balls, their hearts and minds will follow."

"That's not how it went. I slept with him before I knew who he was."

Trish frowned. "Okay, now I'm confused. I thought you saw him at the meeting."

"Well, we got started a little early." And Cilla told them the story of the flat tire and the poolside meet. "So we're flirting like crazy, and the next thing I know, we're up in my room playing strip poker."

"For which you just happened to have a deck of playing cards," Thea said dryly.

"I believe in being prepared," Cilla said haughtily.

"Who won?"

"He did."

"That's convenient," Sabrina observed.

Cilla snorted. "Not even. I wanted to go to bed with him. I didn't necessarily want to be the first one to get naked. He hustled me."

"You know what they say, if a man is good at one thing, he'll be good at another." Delaney's eyes brightened. "Was he good in bed?"

The thought still sent butterflies through Cilla. "He was amazing. I mean, like seeing-God amazing. And that was without even closing the deal. Neither one of us had a condom," she explained.

Kelly stared. "Just foreplay?"

"Well, there's foreplay and then there's foreplay, particularly when you have an inventive man on the premises."

"So what are you going to do now? You have to work together, right?" Paige was nothing if not practical.

Cilla shot her a look. "We have sex on the conference table. What do you think?"

Delaney gave a leer. "Bet the board would love that."

"Seriously, though," Paige pursued, "you're going to have to work this out."

Cilla released a loud breath. "Well, we both agreed it wasn't going to be a problem—to put it behind us. Then again, that was before we found out we were going to be working on this project. That's going to make it kind of hard because we had really great chemistry together."

"You're in a situation where you need all the control you can get," Thea told her. "Sleeping with him's going to put you in a one-down situation."

Delaney snorted. "What planet are you living on? There's no better way to get control of a man than through sex. She plays her cards right, he'll be putty in her hands."

A bearded man walked by their table. His hair had the same sweep to it as Rand's, and that quickly Cilla was back in her room at the hotel, listening to the sounds of the atrium fountain and feeling Rand's hands sliding over her.

"I've got to go to the rest room," Sabrina said. "I'm dying, here. Cilla, no more talking until I get back," she ordered.

As soon as she walked away, Paige leaned forward. "Okay, Cilla, we'll get back to you in a minute, but we've got to talk about Sabrina's shower."

"It's barely even May. Isn't this a little early?" Cilla asked.

"She's getting married at the beginning of July. We need to have the shower next month."

Delaney looked puzzled. "How'd that get pawned off on you, Paige? Kelly, I thought you were best chick."

"Maid of honor."

"Whatever. Aren't you supposed to do that?"

"I'm going to Boston next week with Trish to cover the filming of her script. I figured Paige would do a better job keeping a handle on the details."

"Anyway, we can have it at my house, though I'll need help. Kelly's in charge of getting her over there. We'll have to talk later about the rest of it," Paige said, glancing over her shoulder at the rest room doors.

"Like the toys?" Delaney asked. "Someone's got to go get her something really raunchy."

"I nominate you. I just tried to get a vibrator for another friend's shower and, trust me, it's not the easiest job."

"Don't be so prim, Paige," Delaney chided her. "Just go to an adult toy store."

"What do you think I am, a wimp?" she replied scornfully, adjusting the lapels of her gray silk jacket. "I went to one and it was just gross."

"Offended your delicate design sensibilities?"

"More like offended my infectious disease sensibilities. I wouldn't trust anything that came out of a box there, not with those clerks. We won't even talk about the way it looked."

"Tacky?"

"Not if you like displays of giant dildos, I guess. It was sort of like walking into a *Penthouse* photo spread."

"Look on it as a way to broaden your horizons," Kelly told her.

"I'm all for broadening my horizons, but not when it means carrying a box plastered with naked women up to some drooling guy at the cash register."

Thea frowned. "I'd probably just go to a catalog."

"Don't go there," Cilla warned her.

"Why not? It seems like it would be simpler."

"Not in the long term. They sell your name. I got a vibrator that way one time. A month or two later, all these really explicit adult film catalogs started showing up in my mailbox." Cilla could just imagine what would have happened if her mother had seen one when she was visiting. "And then it got worse, I started getting catalogs for throwing stars and knives, and subscription offers from *Soldier of Fortune.* Apparently, the thinking is that people who like toys are also into porn and violence."

"Thea's right," Paige said. "Why can't normal stores sell them? It shouldn't be that hard in this day and age."

And the wheels began to turn slowly in Cilla's head. Why not, she thought. She was looking for a way to distinguish Danforth Annex from the rest. Danforth Annex, a store about unapologetic sex. Why couldn't they carry a small, discreet line of toys and lotions? Why couldn't they provide a place for women to buy sex products in a comfortable environment?

She tuned back in to the conversation.

"We've been through the sexual revolution and beyond," Thea was saying. "Isn't it time for reputable stores that a person's comfortable going into started stocking some of this stuff?"

"What stuff?" Sabrina asked from behind them.

"Sex toys."

"What brought that up?"

They all looked at one another blankly. "Um, Danforth Annex is going to start carrying them," Paige said hastily. "Isn't that right, Cilla?"

The corners of Cilla's mouth tugged up into a smile. "Sure is."

6

IT REMINDED CILLA of a nightclub, all bright color, flashing lights and loud music. The woman next to Cilla nodded to the beat as she picked up a pewter and gold tank dress knitted in a pattern that looked vaguely Aztec or Mayan or something ancient. It ran about twelve hundred dollars; Cilla knew because she had it hanging in her closet at home.

Par for the course for a Saturday afternoon at Diavala's. Indeed, the crowd that packed the store, or many of its neighbors, for that matter, wasn't a bit shy about plunking down the plastic when they found something they liked. As she'd told the board, the money was out there if a shop had the right chemistry.

She loitered, watching a woman across the shop exclaim over an Anna Sui miniskirt that Cilla had tried unsuccessfully to get Danforth to carry. It was a frivolous pale green dotted with flowers, with flirty ribbons at waistline and hem. The buyer would find a good look, the store would make a few hundred dollars and everybody would be happy. Stifling the perennial urge to browse the rack herself, Cilla walked outside.

She'd spent the previous hour working her way through the shops at the expensive end of hip Melrose

Avenue, and it was almost as though she'd been club hopping. The atmosphere felt that good. And the Danforth Annex atmosphere felt that bad. Cilla pushed through the door and resisted the urge to yawn.

It was the taupe that did it, she thought. The taupe, the ecru, the camel, accented here and there with a daring bit of cream. The window displays alone would have turned her off. The store was silent, the clothing dull, the very air seemed enervated. In a word, boring. The thick carpet underfoot muffled her footsteps, and those of the sales associate, with her smooth French twist and her painfully subtle—taupe—clothing. "May I help you?"

"No thank you, I'm just looking." Cilla roamed through the boutique, a scaled-down carbon copy of the Danforth flagship store. She couldn't figure out how they'd ever thought it would fly. The hushed decor, discreet stock and unobtrusive salesclerks might have worked well in the Rodeo Drive location, where an atmosphere of luxury was the order of the day. Here on Melrose, though, the clientele demanded more: fun, excitement, the unexpected.

And she was going to do her best to give it to them.

The front door opened and a tone sounded—discreet, naturally—as Rand stepped into the shop. Awareness rolled through her. It had been over two weeks since she'd seen him. His hair was a bit longer, his eyebrows straighter than she remembered. He'd come in business casual—khakis and a rough-weave shirt that reminded her of a kilim rug, in earth tones accented with blue and red. It made his shoulders look very solid and wide.

"Fresh off the airplane?" she asked as he walked up,

nodding at his clothes. There was something so sexy about long sleeves rolled up to show a man's forearms, Cilla thought, staring at the sinew and muscle exposed by his shirt.

"It's Saturday," he said easily. "I figured I get time off from suits for good behavior."

"Fair enough." Without thinking, she held out her hand to shake. And heat dragged her back to the mindless urgency of those hours in the desert. It was impossible to block memories tangible enough to have the curl of tension growing within her.

"So what's the plan?" Rand asked.

Cilla blinked. *Focus,* she reminded herself. Whatever was between them, they had a job to do. She took a deep breath. "First we need to get the lay of the land. After we look around here, you should see some of the other shops on the street."

"Already done," he said easily.

It didn't surprise her. Rand Mitchell clearly liked to be prepared. "So you see what we're up against."

"Kind of hard not to." He looked around the store. The salesclerk was staring avidly at him, Cilla noticed with a little frisson of annoyance. He didn't seem to notice his audience. But then again, he wouldn't.

"The look's got to go," she said, starting to drift. "I have a friend who's an interior designer. I'll bring her in for a consult. She can give us something more exciting."

"Have her do an estimate. We'll get a couple more and make a decision then."

"Paige is the right person. Six months, remember? We don't have any time to waste."

He stopped and turned to look at her. "You can

waste time by rushing into things, too." He wandered toward the back of the store where the shoes and handbags were displayed. "I'm sure your friend's a good designer but we've got a lot riding on this. And we've got a budget. Let's think this through."

"Trust me, I have."

"Team project, Cilla," he reminded her. "We've got to agree."

She subsided, fuming. The salesclerk lingered nearby, openly curious, and Cilla gave in. "Fine," she told him. "Let's go grab some lunch and rough out a plan."

THEY SAT BY THE WINDOW in a Vietnamese restaurant and ordered lemon shrimp soup and pad viet. The waiter took their menus and disappeared.

Rand leaned back against his chair and studied Cilla. There was a gloss of sophistication on her today that had been missing in the desert. Then again, she was different every time he saw her. How was it, then, that every time he had to fight the pull of fascination? Whether it was the reckless sexuality of the woman at the resort, the bruised ambition of the woman in the board meeting, or the striking style of the woman sitting across from him, the facets of her personality drew him in.

Enough, he lectured himself. Bad enough that he'd slept with her then. It was patently foolish to get caught up in her now. There was a job to be done, and that was what he needed to focus on. It was one thing to take chances with his personal life; it was something different to take risks professionally.

He'd learned that the hard way.

Rand stirred. "So are we going to be able to work together, here?"

"Why do you ask?"

"I don't think it was what either of us was looking for when we walked into that conference room. You wanted free rein."

"And you wanted to stick with your glam project in Europe. Looks like we both got thrown a curve."

He studied her. "That's right, you were the curve-ball pitcher, weren't you?"

"Don't blame me for this."

"You were the one with the big ideas."

"And you were the one who told them you had a better way."

Their waiter stopped to drop off iced tea for them both. Rand reached out and unwrapped his straw. "Me and my big mouth," he acknowledged. "Like I said at the meeting, I agree with you in this on general principles."

"Good thing, because otherwise it's going to be a pretty hairy six months."

"I also said I wasn't prepared to go as far as you, so why don't you tell me what you've got in mind and we can see how far apart our ideas are."

Irritation flashed in her eyes. She kept control of it, though, he thought with approval. You needed passion about your work to do anything effectively. You needed control for the same reason.

She moistened her lips. "The store needs significant changes to become competitive with the surrounding properties."

"Check."

"Starting with the name."

He shook his head. "We can't afford it. We don't have a budget that's going to cover a remodel and signage, let alone a ground-up rebranding campaign. Besides, Danforth brings a certain cachet."

"The Danforth name is the kiss of death around here. Didn't you see that street? Those shoppers don't want to go to a store they associate with the ladies who lunch."

"It doesn't change our financials."

Cilla considered. "Okay, how about this? We keep Danforth Annex in the places where we can't easily get rid of it, but we shorten it to the Annex in advertising, on bags, anywhere we can. You've got to admit, it's catchier," she said persuasively.

She had a point, he admitted. Short and punchy beat long any day, and the nickname angle worked. "Okay, the Annex, it is. What else?"

"A complete remodel, structure, color, furnishings," she ticked off on her fingers. "The taupe has got to go."

"Taupe? What's taupe?"

"You know, the color of the walls."

"Oh. Beige. Like the carpet."

"No, that's ecru."

Rand frowned. He didn't know what ecru was, but he knew the carpet was beige, just like the walls, just like the island that held the cash register. "You women and your colors," he muttered. "Why don't you just call it what it is?"

"I am. It's ecru."

"Like the couches."

"No, those are camel."

He sat on that one for a minute. "This is really all just a plot," he said finally. "Right? It's like a secret code or something so you can make us guys feel like we're clueless."

She laughed then, and the sound dragged him away from thoughts of business, making him wish it could just be the two of them, finding pleasure in one another's company. Finding pleasure, period.

"It's to pay you back for all the things you stuffed down our shirts in first grade," she told him. "We like to torment you."

The way memories of her had been tormenting him for the past two weeks. "Okay, forget the color thing. Let's get back to your wish list."

"My to-do list," she corrected. "After all, it's basically my project."

"I seem to remember it being handed to both of us, and since we're both responsible for its success or failure, let's call it as it is," he said pleasantly.

The look she shot him this time was more turbulent. And beyond anything, the intensity in her eyes reminded him of the way she looked right before she came.

Before she could say anything, the waiter brought their food. The ceremony of distributing the soup, the mint and basil leaves, the bean sprouts and nuts took several minutes, but finally the waiter left them to eat.

"The store has to have energy," Cilla said, apparently deciding to ignore his comment for now. "That means something special. Paige has a design degree. It's not just about color and fabric for her. She's equally capable of tearing down walls, building in new ones, doing whatever we need to get a really original look."

"And I'm not saying we don't use her. I'm just saying we need to have a couple of people to choose from."

"And *I'm* saying that by the time we get proposals from our field and make our decision, we'll be two months along. The calendar is not our friend right now, and maybe that means we have to do things differently than you'd like." Her eyes challenged him. "Paige has a break between projects right now. She could have us ready to open in two weeks."

She had a point, he admitted grudgingly, but no good manager took someone on blindly. "I want to see her portfolio and a proposal before we do anything. If I like it, we go forward. If we don't agree, we get additional candidates."

"I'll ask Paige for midweek," Cilla promised, "if not sooner."

"Good," Rand nodded, knowing that they'd been talking, literally and figuratively, about window dressing. What really mattered was the store concept. He had a nasty notion that there they diverged wildly. "So now we've got the Annex with our hip new interior. What do we put in it?"

"Sex."

"I'm not sure that's legal." His voice was dry.

She smiled. "You know what I mean, sexy clothes, sexy salesclerks, sexy music. Sex. Things that will get people talking."

"You mentioned Versace, Gaultier."

"Sure, and Helmut Lang and Vivienne Westwood.

We want to be the place the hot young things in Hollywood come to get their clothes."

"It's a great concept, but that can't be it."

"Sure it can."

"No. Fifty percent revenue jump, remember? We can't subsist on superstar couture," he argued. "We need to have a broader spectrum."

"Then you're right back where we started from." He knew she wasn't pouting, but he had to remind himself to stop staring at that mouth of hers. "Stewart Law had a really brilliant idea with putting a store on Melrose," she continued, "but then he lost his nerve and tried to play it too safe. You saw where that got him."

"I also know you can play it too far the other way." He knew it only too well. "Look, we're agreed that we want the hot, marquee designers. That's the merchandise that will define the store, that will make people want to come in." He played with the wrapper to his straw, thinking out loud. "But maybe we draw in the average Jane. The image attracts her. She's got money but she's not wild enough for our exact target demographic. If we can have a few less edgy things for her— some Narciso Rodriguez, some Jil Sander—then she goes away happy. More important, she comes back."

"Jil Sander, huh?" She studied him.

"Yep."

"How can you know Jil Sander and not know what color ecru is?"

"There are some kinds of information my mind is incapable of dealing with."

"Fragile flower."

"Indeed. Now, you mentioned using the store as a launch pad for a lingerie line you're starting."

Her face lit and his heart rate bumped up. "I've been working on it for almost a year and we're just about ready to roll it out. Imagine the kind of coverage we could get, 'Danforth heiress launches lingerie line at hot new Annex.'"

"Got it all worked out, have you?"

"If you're not two steps ahead, you're one behind," she observed, nibbling on a bean sprout.

He watched her. "Good point."

"I've got contacts in all of the mainstream fashion magazines, as well as the L.A. papers. We could even hold a runway show here to generate some buzz. Think of it, the Annex as exclusive outlet for Cilla D."

"It's good that you're being so selfless about this."

"Look, it's good exposure for the line, I know that, but it's also a way around our marketing budget," she said reasonably. "People love exclusive anything, and let's face it, they love an heiress. Let's give them what they want."

"How about if we keep it under consideration for now. You thinking about anything else?"

"Yes."

"And that would be."

She stared at him and something flickered in her eyes, something that had a slow curl of tension twisting inside him.

"I've been thinking about sex."

His mouth was suddenly dry with forbidden desire, and all the blood in his body headed south. Jumping back into their affair was the last thing they should be doing. Logically, he knew that. So why was he finding it so hard to remember?

"The clothing isn't enough. The atmosphere isn't enough. We need something that will make us different."

She was talking about the store, he realized, letting out a breath of mixed disappointment and relief. "Go on."

She leaned forward. "Let's take it one step further. Let's go out on the edge, get word of mouth like you wouldn't believe."

Something about her tone brought up his guard. "What do you have in mind?"

"Toys." She blinked at him guilelessly. "Sex toys."

"Out of the question."

"What do you mean out of the question?" Her chin rose. "Just listen before you go ruling things out. I can convince you."

"That'll be a trick."

"Just listen, will you? I was talking with my friends about it a couple of nights ago. There's not really any place comfortable to buy them. The places that don't look like they'd give you a disease generally have a really boring selection."

"Horrors."

"Hey, if a woman's getting up her nerve to buy a toy, she ought to at least be able to get what she wants." Cilla thought about it a moment. "Look, we could stick them in the back with the lingerie, maybe in a curtained-off area. This will work, trust me."

"Sure, but how many customers will we lose in the meantime?"

"Just think of it," she went on, ignoring him. "The fabled back room at the Annex, for the discerning buyer. I know the right people to talk to to send the word around. Your customer who walks away with the Jil Sander will never even know about it."

And he could just imagine how this would go over at Danforth. "Exactly what do you think the board is going to say if they find out the Annex is selling sex toys?"

"We don't tell them." She shrugged. "We don't even tell the press. By the time the board finds out we'll be making money off it and there's no way they'll interrupt it."

"Oh, yeah? Christ, your father would have a fit. I'd be out of a job before you could say vibrator."

Her lips twitched. "Are you afraid of my father?"

"No, but I've got a career, here."

"Like I said, we don't tell them until after we have the revenue numbers to support it."

"Assuming we don't get blown out of the water before."

"Come into the twenty-first century, Rand. It's not like we'd be running a prostitution ring," she said, amused. "They're just sex toys. People really aren't going to care all that much."

"You say."

"Do a quick marketing poll," she invited him. "Better yet, go to the *Cosmo* Web site and look at their annual sex survey. You're going to see that the average twentysomething woman likes her toys and likes her pleasure." She studied him. "If I'd had toys with me that night at the resort, would they have turned you off or would you have used them?"

His imagination exploded with the image. And he saw the secret, satisfied smile slide over her face.

"You see? Toys have a place. I think we'll be fine."

"I want to do some research on it," he warned her.

She rose. "You do that."

CILLA LAY IN THE BATH that night, letting the hot water and bubbles work away at her tension.

They'd stuck her with a baby-sitter who was supposed to keep her from doing anything edgy that might alarm the Danforth customer. Unfortunately, the company had tried that approach with the Annex and gotten precisely nowhere. Why couldn't they understand that it had to be different?

Why couldn't Rand?

All right, she grudgingly admitted, he was at least open to some of her ideas, and behind others, but he kept having these odd flashes of conservatism. He kept playing it safe.

And she couldn't figure out why. The guy she'd met at the resort had been ready and willing to take chances, she thought, remembering their dawn foray to slide naked into one of the hot springs and touch each other in the fizzing water. She didn't get the feeling that he'd been jumping out of character, either, especially since it had been his idea.

He seemed to understand the purpose of her direction with the Annex and realize the potential for success. And yet, periodically, he'd pull back, like a dog walking up to an invisible fence. Maybe he'd been so burned by the dot-com crash that he'd become leery of risk, turning his back on what had made him successful to begin with. And in a company like Danforth, being risk averse was rewarded.

She soaped up the loofah and rubbed it moodily over her shoulder. So say that Rand Mitchell was truly forgetting—or trying to forget—who he was. He couldn't walk away from it entirely. He hadn't, that much she knew. She'd seen him without inhibitions, she'd seen him taking chances.

And she couldn't be around him without wanting him.

She wanted to succeed professionally, and she couldn't do that without making the Annex fly. To make the Annex fly, she needed Rand to loosen up.

Okay, strategy change. Maybe all she really needed to do was remind him of who he really was. And if that took seducing him, well, she prided herself on being a woman who did what was necessary.

Cilla began to hum, a smile of anticipation spreading across her face.

7

PAIGE LOOKED ACROSS the store, her eyes calm and assessing. "What I'm seeing for the Annex is modern, clean design, but with an edge." She turned to Cilla and Rand. "That's what you need."

The three of them stood at the cash register area at the back of the store. Sunlight spilled in the front windows, dulled almost immediately by the deadened tones. Cilla wished she had Paige's sense for design and could envision it already made over and fresh looking. Since she didn't, the next best thing was having Paige herself, who looked every bit the successful design professional in her sleek white suit and the perfect blond arcs of her haircut.

"The first thing we do is get rid of the neutrals and bring in some more open colors."

"Something bright," Cilla put in, looking around at the dispirited walls of the Annex.

Paige shook her head. "You're not going to crowd the space with racks the way you would the Forth's women's department, are you?"

"No. I want people to be able to see the clothes," Cilla told her.

"Exactly. We want to carry that sensibility through

in the design, too. Don't let the colors overpower what you're selling."

"Ditch the ecru, though."

Rand stirred. "I thought it was taupe." Today, he wore a beautifully cut Armani that brought out the blue in his eyes.

"Let's just call it gone," Paige said with a smile. "I'm thinking sleek minimalist with a touch of retro. Hard, glossy floor coverings, maybe build in some recessed segments and isolate your color there." She laid out sketches on the counter behind the cash registers and they crowded in to look.

Cilla could feel Rand's proximity, even though he wasn't touching her. It made her mouth dry to think of what might happen between them.

"What about furnishings?" Rand asked, moving slightly away from Cilla as though their closeness made him uneasy.

"Le Corbusier chairs," Paige replied promptly. "Maybe a couple of van der Rohe Barcelona couches, that sort of thing. Mix up the colors. You want to encourage people to get comfortable. The more bodies you have, the more excitement."

Rand nodded, Cilla saw with a satisfied smile. She'd known Paige would convince him. There was no one in the world who could present her judgment as confidently as Paige. Cilla stared at the sketches and then at the store, trying to imagine it transformed.

"So, I had this idea about the wall art," Paige said now. "What about making the space a sort of mini art gallery? I mean real art, not match-your-couch art," she elaborated quickly. "Focus on local rising stars, make the Annex not just the place to go for the latest clothes but for the latest visual media, too. You enhance your decor without cost outlay, and up your coolness quotient about three thousand percent."

Cilla felt an unholy stir of excitement in the pit of her stomach. This was what she wanted for the Annex, something special, something you can't miss. "What do you think, Rand? I could have a little chat with the owner of the gallery that shows Ty's work, see if we could collaborate."

In his eyes, she saw her certainty reflected—this was right for the project, dead on in every respect. He nodded. "Do it."

"So what's your availability as far as the renovation goes, Paige?"

"I basically have the next two weeks free and then I'm locked in to a remodel job for a longtime customer."

"Can you get this done in two weeks?"

She gave Cilla a pitying smile. "I never bid on a job I can't hold to schedule."

"I should have known better than to ask." Cilla grinned. "In that case, how soon can you start?"

"How soon is now?" Paige gathered together her sketches and tucked them into her portfolio. "I checked in with my contractors when I worked up the proposal. Let me verify their availability and I'll get back to you with a final timeline." She zipped the gray leather folio shut. "You're going to want to shut down beginning next Monday because I'll have the builders and painters making a mess all over."

"We'll take care of it," Cilla assured her.

"She's definitely the right one," Rand said, watching Paige head to the door, pulling out her cell phone as she walked.

Cilla cleared her throat. "I'm sorry, did you say something?" she asked him politely.

He gave her a dark look. "You're one of those, huh?"

"One of what?"

"One of those 'I told you so' types?"

Cilla stuck her tongue in her cheek. "Well, if it'll make your ego feel better if we pretend you were on board the whole time, then far be it from me to blow your bliss." She gave him a bright, false smile. "Isn't it lucky that we both realized what a fine job Paige would do from the beginning?"

"Yeah, yeah, yeah, enjoy it."

"I intend to," she told him with a grin.

RAND STUDIED the schedule that Cilla laid out in front of him. "So, step one is the face-lift."

"With the store shut down and a nice Closed For Renovations, Reopening On… sign in the front. We should get a graffiti artist to do it, maybe, painted on plywood."

"It'll cost."

"More targeted than ads," she countered.

There was something different about her today that he couldn't quite put his finger on, something that made him more aware of her than ever before. Her look belonged on Carnaby Street, circa 1964, the skirt very short, the sweater very tight. Her hair was slicked back behind her ears for an almost boyish effect. It made her look anything but, though, all big eyes and lush mouth. Precisely as she'd planned, he was betting.

"It's spending that makes sense," Cilla continued.

She had great instincts, he thought—when she wasn't being outrageous. "You're right. Okay, next, we upgrade the stock."

"Let fun and sex be your watchwords."

"Every waking moment," he said dryly. "We open two and a half weeks from today."

"More or less. And then, we have our grand opening."

"Cost," he reminded her. "We'll already have had our opening."

"Doesn't count. We need to have a special event where we do it up right."

"Why not the day we start business?"

"Too early," she explained. "Too much can go wrong. We need time to get our act in gear, get the buzz going. When all the clerks are trained and everything's going like clockwork, *that's* when we have our grand opening."

"Which, I take it, you've already scheduled."

A smile hovered around the corners of her mouth. "Five weeks after we open our doors. Four weeks to work the bugs out, then the following week we hold a couple of mini press events, including a champagne reception."

"Invitation only, I hope," he said with a glance toward the racks of thousand dollar merchandise.

"We'll have a very select guest list," Cilla assured him. "Music, finger food, goody bags. Invite the fashion press, as well as some Hollywood A-listers we hope will become our clients."

"To know us is to love us?"

"Something like that." She rose and walked a short distance down the center of the store, her enthusiasm inviting him to join her in some devilish fun. "I was even thinking we could put in a temporary runway and have a show that night," she said over her shoulder, then turned and walked back to him, looking leggy and delicious. Leggy and delicious and…clever, he realized. That was what made her hard to ignore, the combination of sassy and savvy.

Work, he reminded himself. "Who are you going to invite to show?"

"A couple of the locals we'll be carrying." She shot him a cagey look. "And maybe Cilla D."

"Ah, yes, we need to talk about that."

She dropped down onto the couch next to him and he caught a hint of her scent. "Things have been going so well, Rand. Don't turn into a spoilsport."

"Let's talk about it back in the office." He needed to get back into the boring conservative surroundings because being alone with Cilla Danforth was fast tempting him to do things that were completely out of the question.

Like kissing her senseless.

"Back to the office, hmm?" Cilla nibbled on her lower lip. "Of course, since I drove here to begin with, that means you're appealing to my good nature to get you back?"

"Who was the one who volunteered? 'My little car will be easier to park, Rand'?"

"I was trying to be public spirited. It's not my fault you drive a giant gas guzzler. Anyway, I think if you want to get back to work, you'd be smart to be open to my suggestions."

"I said we'd talk about it," he reminded her as they rose.

"I SUPPOSE THAT MEANS the jury's still out on the toys, too," Cilla said as she unlocked the passenger door for Rand and walked around to get in herself. She reached into the space behind her seat with one hand to rummage through her attaché case.

"I'm still waiting to be convinced that the benefits outweigh the possibility of negative publicity," Rand said. It came out more old-maidish than he'd intended, but he wasn't about to let her push the project off the rails.

Cilla tossed a file folder into his lap and pulled into traffic.

"What's this?" He opened it to see some pages torn from a magazine and clipped together. From a women's magazine, he realized, or, rather, *the* magazine for young, hip single women. "Baby Don't Stop— What You Love In Bed?"

"I thought you might be interested in seeing the results of the latest sex survey. Take a look at question fifteen, which shows the percentage of women who have purchased sex toys." She punched on the radio and turned it down low.

"Are you telling me their readers are our demographic?" he asked in disbelief.

"Why not? Just because they've got money doesn't mean they don't enjoy sexy stories. Wealthy women read magazines, too, you know."

"You don't say." Rand skimmed the pages as she drove. "So it's true that size counts, hmm?"

"If we're being honest, yes, but only to a point." Cilla pulled to a stop at a red light and flicked a glance at his hands. "Trust me, big boy, you've got nothing to worry about. Any other surprises there for you?"

"The missionary position is number one?"

"There's a lot to be said for missionary. I'd be happy to show you, if you like," she offered, with a hot, silky smile that had his hair curling.

A beat went by. Slowly, Rand let his breath out. "I thought we agreed that wasn't a good idea."

Cilla slanted him a look. "I think maybe we need to revisit that decision."

"What's that supposed to mean?"

"Well, if we're both professionals, why can't we do what we want to in our spare time?" She glanced over her shoulder and changed lanes.

He could think of a million reasons why they shouldn't. He could think of one reason why they should: he knew how good it would be. That wasn't enough, but God, he wanted her.

He stared at her, trying to formulate a reply, and then took a better look at the street they were driving down. "Where the hell are you going? I thought we were heading back to the office."

"We'll get there eventually," she said breezily.

"And in the meantime?"

Cilla gave him a smile he didn't trust. "Consider it a field trip."

They were heading down Fairfax, on a block where

more windows had bars than not. She turned into a strip mall with an adult bookstore.

"No," he said flatly.

"Don't worry, we're not stopping." She patted his knee and pulled back out onto the road. "It's just to give you an idea of the options out there for your average woman who wants some sexy playthings." Cilla headed up and over onto Santa Monica. "I don't care how bad she wants it, she's not going to go into a place like that without a decontamination suit."

"There are other options."

"Sure. Catalogs, but who wants to offer up their name, address, credit card, the works?"

"I mean more reputable stores that sell sex toys."

"Sure." She whipped off the street into a parking lot. "Like this."

The brick-red building sat isolated in its own parking lot, edged with sandy rectangles sprouting mostly weeds. The sign on the roof said The Pleasure Zone.

Cilla opened her door. "Let's go shopping."

She was in high good humor, he noticed. He didn't get over to West Hollywood very often, but he had a pretty good idea of what lay inside. A combination sex shop and head shop, he figured.

And he was right.

Inside, the colors were dark and incense lay heavy on the air. The store looked maybe a bit on the tawdry side, admittedly, but clean enough. Certainly nothing that would alarm the average woman shopper. Okay, so maybe he felt a little bit awkward, but that was primarily because most of the toys were for women or for guys who batted for the other team. It wasn't exactly a place he belonged.

"So what's wrong with this?" he asked.

"Well, it's not exactly the kind of store the average trust-fund baby is used to."

He shrugged. "It'll be good for them to get a glimpse of what real life is like."

"We stick with that idea and we're walking away from revenue." She passed a wire book rack and stopped to pull out a volume. "Oh, look—*Going Down on a Woman: the complete guide*. Nothing you need," she told him and put it back on the shelf.

There it was again, that disturbing challenge, that reminder of what had passed between them. What was still between them. If he were smart, he'd let it go.

But a part of him itched to take her up on it.

Cilla gave him a careless glance and blithely continued down the aisle to a display of lotions and oils. "Now, see, we could carry some of this stuff. Not even you could kick up a fuss about this."

Rand frowned. It wasn't as if he was some kind of uptight moralist. He just wasn't convinced it was going to sell and he wasn't sure it was worth the risk. Then again...

Cilla picked up a sample bottle of almond oil and sniffed it, then rubbed some on the inside of her wrist. "This smells wonderful. Try it," she invited, holding her hand up to him.

He caught the scent, the rich, sweet fragrance that emanated from her skin as though she were some luscious dessert. It smelled delectable. *She* smelled delectable, and he had a fleeting urge to press his lips to the fragile skin.

Cilla dropped her arm as though she hadn't noticed and continued down the aisle. "Oh, now here's one we should definitely have," she said, reading the label. "Hot friction oil." Delighted, she rubbed a bit of it into the back of her hand. Her mouth parted in pleasure. "This, you've got to feel." Before he understood her intent, she applied some to the back of his own hand.

He couldn't say whether the heat was from the action of the lotion or the touch of her fingers. Her thumb circled against his skin, heating it, sensitizing it, and—

And he felt himself getting hard.

Okay, this was a problem. Trying to not think about sex around Cilla was a challenge at the best of times. Trying to avoid thinking about it in a store filled with lingerie and sex toys, while she was rubbing hot oil on his hand, was almost impossible.

"All right, I get the point," he said brusquely.

Amusement danced in her eyes. She wasn't upset. She knew exactly why he was reacting the way he was.

And it was just what she wanted.

"So we can at least agree that the lotions and oils make sense, right? A small, discreet display of them?" She picked up a bottle of strawberry-flavored gel and applied a sample to the inside of the wrist without the almond oil. "Hmm," she said, tasting it experimentally. "I don't know. What do you think?" She held it up for him.

Rand looked at her.

"Oh, come on, don't be stuffy about it. Just tell me what you think. It tastes too much like candy for me. Here, try."

Rand bent over her wrist and touched his tongue to

the skin. A burst of sweetness rolled through him. Underneath, though, was the far more enticing flavor of Cilla herself, a taste he had already learned and tried to forget.

Tried and failed.

His lips lingered. He heard Cilla's soft intake of breath, felt her tremble. He knew he needed to release her, but seconds passed before he could make himself do it.

When he looked up, her eyes were a little hazy. "Well, maybe we'll skip those, try some others," Cilla said, her voice a little uneven. "Let's keep going."

She drifted away slowly at first, gaining purpose as she moved. "Ah yes, here we are," she said, her voice back to normal.

This was where the store got serious, he saw, looking over the array of typical, recognizable or frankly mysterious gadgets that sat on the shelf. The dildos, he recognized.

He lifted one. "Instant boyfriend?"

"It takes more than that to make a boyfriend," Cilla shot back at him and went on to the vibrators.

"I'd have thought a woman like you would have one or two of these already," he said, watching her switch on a sleek silver model and test it against her hand.

"I do," she laughed, pressing the vibrating tip against his chest. "I don't use it all that much, though."

The buzz went through his sternum. The look in her eyes set up an answering resonance much farther down. "Oh yeah? Why's that?"

"Well, let's face it, it's not exactly something that a real man can do, is it?"

"Yeah, so?"

She stepped in close to him. "So I'd rather stick with the one hundred percent pure, organic version, thanks very much."

Before he could react, she'd moved away and had begun working her way along the aisle. "Now as I see it, we should have a couple of types of vibrators—your anatomically correct and your basic smooth versions. I think we should skip the artsy ones," she added, flicking a disdainful hand at a gizmo that looked, near as he could tell, like a dildo with a two inch tall rabbit attached at the base.

"And what's that, the multitasker?"

"For the girl who wants everything." She picked it up and turned it on. "You've never seen one of these before?"

"Not ones shaped like rabbits, no. Anyway, I don't exactly study them. They're all basically for your gang anyway."

"Oh, you'd be surprised at what it could do for you, sugar," she purred at him, leaning it to press it for an instant against his crotch. The vibration sent a jolt through his system. "Like I said before," she whispered, "you've been hanging around with the wrong crowd."

His hard-on was immediate. Rand resisted the urge to look around like some high school kid and see who'd seen them. "You always like public games?"

"I seem to remember you did, too."

He had a sense of fighting a losing battle. "Whatever happened to taking care of business?"

"Nothing says we can't do both, as long as we're smart about it."

Her eyes were dark with promise as she leaned in toward him. Her scent wound around his brain, taking him back to the hot, urgent moments in the desert, the taste of her, the feel of her heat.

Rand dove his hands into her hair and dragged her to him.

Frustration. Desire. Compulsion. The wanting swept through him like a fury, finding release in the hard, bruising pressure of his mouth on hers. Her taste bloomed against his tongue, sweet, spicy and darkly seductive. He poured into the kiss the longing and the denial he'd felt for three long weeks, every time he'd seen her, every time he'd sat across from her in a meeting room, heard her laughing voice.

Every time he'd dreamed of her.

They were in the middle of a store and he didn't give a damn. They were working together and for a moment he didn't care. She matched him, took him deeper, her arms wrapping around him, her body pressing close.

Somehow, somewhere, in some small pocket of sanity he still possessed, he realized he was flirting with disaster. Somewhere, he knew he had to find a way to stop. Torturously, he began clawing his way back from the brink.

They parted, breathing hard, Cilla's eyes enormous and dark.

"We are not going to do this," he said evenly.

"After that? You've got to be kidding."

"It's not smart, Cilla, for either of us." He turned to leave the store, with her following him.

"Y'all come back, now," the guy behind the counter called.

CILLA SLAPPED OPEN the doors and stomped out into the sunlight of the parking lot. "What the hell was that all about in there," she demanded. "What are you playing at?"

"What am I playing at? What about you, with your lotions and vibrators?"

"That was me trying to seduce you. I'd think you'd be smart enough to recognize it. I don't see why it has to be so hard. I want you, you want me. We're adults. We ought to be able to keep the two separate," she flared, marching to her car.

"You can't possibly be that naive," he snapped back. "We have an affair, it ends one way or another, and then we've got to work together? No way am I walking into that."

She shoved her key into the lock. "Haven't you ever heard of casual sex, Rand? Trust me, I don't want to have your children. I just want to have a good time."

"That's not a good enough reason," he said from behind her.

"Oh, no?" She spun on her heel. "Then how about this?"

If the earlier kiss had sizzled, this one flamed. His hands ran down her body. Her fingers tangled in his hair. Through the alchemy of emotion, anger and lust fused to become molten desire. Mouth to mouth, body to body, they met. They sought provocation, not tenderness, challenge, not kindness. The flare, the fire satisfied in a way nothing else could have.

The honk of a passing car brought them to their senses.

Cilla leaned back against the car, breathing hard. "If you think you can put that away in a tidy little box, you're dreaming." She touched a finger to her bruised lips. "It's going to happen, Rand. You might as well get used to it."

8

"WHAT ARE YOU swinging at?" Rand demanded of the television in disgust. He sprawled on the black leather couch in a faded Batman T-shirt and jeans, watching the Anaheim Angels fight off the Tampa Bay Devil Rays. Two feet away, in a nearly identical position, sat his oldest friend, Wayne Castle.

They'd grown up together in Anaheim, down in Orange County, playing Little League, worshiping the Angels, riding their bicycles to the stadium and to the beach when they weren't in school. Moving on to college and employment hadn't interfered with their friendship. Rand earned degrees at Cal Berkeley and Stanford, and headed east to conquer the business world. Wayne became a dentist and returned to Costa Mesa to practice. It was a rare week when they didn't talk, and if it was mostly about sports, they somehow always managed to weave in the fabric of their lives at the same time.

Eckstein hit a line drive that went through the glove of the Tampa Bay shortstop, allowing the Angel on third to score.

Wayne clapped. "Yes, thank you. We accept charity in all of its manifestations."

"There's no way they should be fighting this hard with Tampa," Rand muttered bad temperedly. Tampa Bay held the spot similar to the one the Angels had back when Rand was a kid—the cellar. Being an Angel fan back then had been a matter of learning a tolerance for pain. The occasional winning seasons had always ultimately ended in heartbreak, until he'd given up hope and just settled for dogged loyalty. Then had come the miraculous 2002 season, with its World Series win. Pretty much anytime after that, Rand figured, he could die a happy man.

Vladimir Guerrero swung at a hanging curveball and sent it arcing high out over the back fence of the park and toward the freeway. "Goodbye, Mr. Spaulding," Wayne hollered as another man came home.

"Only two runs behind, now." Rand took a swig of beer and lapsed back on the couch.

Wayne gave him a stare. "So what's put you in the great mood today?"

"What do you mean?"

"What do I mean, he asks," Wayne said to an invisible person in the room. "You haven't exactly been Mr. Personality, and you're on your third beer, which I don't think I've seen you do in about ten years."

"They were getting past their freshness date."

"And, so are you. What's going on?"

Tampa Bay made a pitching change and the game broke.

"Oh, I've just got some things that are being a pain in the butt," Rand muttered with a scowl.

"Work things or woman-type things?"

"Yes."

"Ah. The dreaded mix."

Rand tapped his fingers restlessly on the couch. "Cilla's pushing me to sleep with her. No strings, she says."

"You're the only guy I know who'd consider that a problem."

"Wayne?" Rand turned to give him a look. "How long have you been having sex?"

Wayne grinned. "Can I count that time with Debbie Foster on the Little League field?"

"That wasn't sex, that was groping."

"She told me it was sex."

"That's what you get for being gullible. How long?" he persisted.

Wayne counted in his head, stopping for a swig of his Sierra Nevada. "Eighteen years." He brightened. "My sex life can vote now."

"And in all of that time, have you ever once had sex with a woman when there were no strings attached?"

Wayne squinted at the ceiling and considered. Finally, he shook his head. "Absolutely not."

"Exactly. She might say it's just for sex, and maybe she even believes it, but it's not. Women don't do sex without strings, and in this case the strings are tangled up around my job."

"Hell, she's going to inherit someday. Maybe it should have some strings for you."

"I'm not sure it doesn't already." Moodily, he took a swig of his beer. "Goddammit, it pisses me off that she is who she is. I like this woman, a lot. If things were different, I'd be all over her."

"So can you hold her off for six months?"

"I'm not sure I can hold myself off for six months."

A commercial came on and Wayne grabbed the remote to switch to ESPN. "Well, one could ask why you care. It's just a six-month project. Besides, you've been telling me since day one that this Danforth gig is a short-term thing for you."

"Short-term is relative. I'm sure as hell not going to make a dumb move based on a short timeline and wind up being screwed if I need it to last longer."

"So you're going to avoid getting screwed to avoid getting screwed."

"You've got a wonderful way with words."

"Thanks, I've been working on it," Wayne said modestly. "Seriously, though, once this project is out of the way, you go on to other stuff, right?"

"Yeah, but—"

"Yeah, but what? You want her. She wants you. Say you take advantage of it. You've got a built-in fail-safe, right? No matter if you crash and burn, you're out of each other's hair in six months. What's the harm?"

"The harm is that maybe I get too cute for my own good." Rand lapsed into moody silence, not reacting even when an error on the Angels' third baseman allowed two Tampa runs to score.

"You know, there are a million beautiful women in L.A.," Wayne said thoughtfully as the camera panned over the crowd. "Look at her, she's a goddess. Hell, if your gut's telling you to stay out of it, then stay out of it." He turned to look at Rand. "You've got the cool apartment. Make use of it. Play around. It'll get her right out of your head."

That was the problem, Rand thought. There might

be a million beautiful women in L.A., but he'd stopped noticing them. Somehow, they'd all just turned into wallpaper. Only Cilla stood out to him. Only Cilla stayed in his mind, hour after hour, day after day.

RAND SAT IN HIS OFFICE typing an answer to an e-mail, trying to figure out how it had already gotten to be 3:00 p.m. At a rap on his open door, he glanced up to see Cilla.

She wore a blue tweed blazer belted over a pencil skirt, and sky-high heels. What was it about a woman in stilettos that was so damned hot, he wondered as he looked at her standing there. But was it the heels or was it the way she stood there like a world-beater, a sexy world-beater, and daring him not to notice?

"Sorry I missed our meeting this morning. Got some time now?"

"Yeah, sure, come on in," he said briskly, focusing back in on business. "What do you need?"

She walked to his client chair and sat, as smoothly and carelessly sultry as Lauren Bacall in one of her movies with Bogie. "I'm starting to pull together inventory for the Annex. I thought we should touch base."

"You're the buyer."

"This isn't exactly about clothing." She crossed her legs with a whisper of hosiery. They were long and lovely, and he had no business staring at them.

But he did.

Cilla smiled. "I've got some more information on the toys." She flicked a glance over her shoulder. "Maybe I should show you instead of telling you."

She rose and circled behind his desk to lay a folder

in front of him. "Here are my recommendations, based on feedback from an informal focus group."

Looking at the list—and in some cases photos—of sex toys didn't turn him on. Having Cilla a foot away from him did. She kept her distance, didn't lean over him obviously, but somehow that made him all the more aware.

Somehow, it made him want her all the more.

"I've got to get some orders out today for what we're going to need going forward," she continued, "especially for the grand opening."

He'd come to the reluctant conclusion that she was right about the toys, so long as they presented them discreetly. They'd have to be careful about the selection, though. He picked up a pen. "I'd cut this, and this," he said briefly, ticking them off.

"Oh, come on, you're taking out the best stuff."

"Let's see how we make out with the basic selection and a couple of edgy items. If they're a success, we can take it further. Slow and gradual is the best way to go."

She looked at him from under her lashes. "I'll remember that."

He had a funny feeling she wasn't talking about merchandise.

"Anyway," she continued, "we need to also make a decision on whether we're going to carry Cilla D. or not, because I've got to get the production house working on it."

The lingerie. Of course. "So take a seat and let's decide." He caught her fleeting smile and realized he'd made a strategic error by letting her know she'd gotten to him. "So why did you start designing, anyway? Nobody at the meeting acted like they knew about it."

"Not a lot of people do." She turned in front of the chair and sat. "It's something I've been doing on the side."

"To keep yourself out of trouble?"

"I never run from trouble." The wicked look she slanted at him shivered down to his toes. "I just couldn't find the kind of lingerie I wanted."

"What kind is that?"

"Something that's drop-dead sexy without being tacky. Hotter than Chantelle, classier than Frederick's of Hollywood. Most designer lingerie is beautiful, but rarely sexy. That's the niche I want."

"G-strings with class?"

"If you like."

He wasn't sure she needed lingerie to look drop-dead sexy, but he figured it probably wasn't appropriate to mention. He was a minimalist. When it came to lingerie, his vote would be nothing at all.

"The Annex is the perfect launch point for the line," Cilla was saying.

He dragged his attention back to the conversation. "That's great for the line, but how do we know it'll fit with the store as a whole?"

Cilla gave him a bold stare. "Sex, remember? It'll fit with the store, trust me."

"I want to look it over before we make a decision," he said finally. He knew, though he didn't say it, that Sam Danforth would be looking particularly hard at their decision to carry the lingerie. Rand wanted to be sure he made the right call.

He'd expected her to take offense. Instead she

looked like a cat in front of a dish of cream. "I'd be happy to show you the whole line."

"Fine. I'll look forward to that." Inwardly, he sighed with relief. "Are we done here?"

Cilla gazed at him, eyes wide. "I thought you wanted to see it."

"Just drop off the file to me."

"I don't have any decent photos, and the sketches are all in New York with the manufacturers. Besides, you don't want to see my renderings," she said silkily. "You want to see the real thing. I've got some samples I can show you."

He had the sudden sense that he'd stumbled into quicksand. Then again, he'd had that same sensation since he'd met Cilla. "You have them here?"

She laughed. "Not here, here. Cilla D. is my gig, not Danforth business. We'll have to go to my Cilla D. office."

"Where's that?"

She rose. "At my house, of course."

And Rand knew he was in big trouble.

"HOW'D YOU WIND UP HERE?" Rand asked as they came up the brick walk to Cilla's twenties Brentwood bungalow. "I'd have expected you to live in Westwood Village or somewhere." Somewhere hipper, more happening, he thought, as he started to follow her up the front steps.

"There you go again, Rand, setting up expectations." She'd taken off her jacket once they'd left the office. With her hair tousled from the ride and the creamy silk camisole she'd worn underneath, she looked inviting and just a bit reckless.

She unlocked the door and walked inside. Rand hesitated before entering. It was going to take some fancy footwork to look at her designs and get out without the two of them doing something they'd be sorry for, he knew that. Why hadn't he just told her to bring the box of lingerie in to the office?

He snorted at himself. Yeah, sure. He could just imagine Sam Danforth walking in on that particular meeting. On the other hand…

"Why don't you grab the box and we can just take it to the store and go through it?"

Cilla turned and walked back toward him, not stopping until they were practically nose to nose. "Why, Rand, a person would think you were afraid to be alone with me," she purred.

"I'm just trying to be efficient."

"And I don't believe you." She tossed her keys into a bowl that sat on the entryway table. "Anyway, we're here. Let's just do it. You can spare that much time, can't you?"

Time, he had. Self-control was steadily decreasing in supply.

Cilla set her purse down. "Can I get you something to drink?"

"No, I'm fine, thanks."

"Feel free to have a seat and I'll go get the goods."

He was happier roaming, looking at the place that she called home. The floors were polished hardwood, the walls plastered, the colors surprisingly calming. The feeling was one of comfort rather than high style. It took him by surprise. He'd expected killing sophistication, not casual, even worn, chic. Perhaps after her high-energy days, Cilla Danforth needed a haven to relax in.

It made him like her all the more.

He walked through an arch into the dining room and its view out into the leafy backyard. Here, her love of color showed through in the confusion of hues from flowering shrubs and beds of pink, orange, red and purple blossoms jammed together in splashy confusion.

A hot tub and pool provided an island of blue amid the greens and warm colors. They'd fooled around in the water at the resort, he remembered, and flashed back to holding her wet and naked against him, sliding his fingers into her heat.

"Did I lose you?" Cilla called.

"Just checking out your backyard," he replied, turning toward the living room.

And stopped dead.

She stood framed in the arch, wearing a fire-engine red teddy, high heels, and nothing else.

His mouth went dry. "I didn't realize this was going to be a fashion show," he blurted, feeling his cock slide against the fabric of his trousers as it twitched. Maybe a better man than he could have torn his eyes away from the slender lines of her body, the way the heels made her legs seem to end somewhere around her neck. Rand couldn't make himself do anything but stare for long minutes.

Cilla's mouth curved. "You can't possibly get an idea of the way lingerie looks when it's on the hanger. If we were in New York, we could have arranged a model, but out here, we've just got to wing it," she said with insincere regret, giving a model's turn. "I didn't think you'd mind. After all, it's not like you haven't seen me naked before."

Water, Rand thought. He just needed to get a glass of water and a seat and he could get through this. He walked toward Cilla. She merely watched him approach until he stood right in front of her. "I take it this is style number one?"

"I figured I'd start off with the easy stuff."

Unable to help himself, Rand reached out and traced a fingertip down the red silk over her hip. "Nice," he commented, watching her nostrils flare as she sucked in a breath. "I'm going to get a drink and take a seat."

"I can see how you might want to," she said, and turned to another archway, presumably to change.

Rand searched for a glass in the kitchen. He wasn't even going to bother telling himself if he were smart he'd leave, because if he were smart, he'd never have come here. He was here because he wanted her, and he was willing to take big risks for it.

He'd known it was coming all along, because the reality was there was no way the two of them were going to walk away from the chemistry they'd had, work or no work. He couldn't escape it, he couldn't hope to evade it. All he could do was try to delay it, to do what was best for both of them.

He wasn't sure he'd even manage that much.

He shucked off his jacket and tie so that he could breathe. By the time she came out again, he'd found water and the couch and at least a fraction of his composure. He was as prepared as he was going to be, he figured. She couldn't have more than three or four more outfits to try on. He hoped.

More than that and she'd have him begging on his knees.

"Are you ready?" Cilla called and walked through the archway.

It was blue this time, a deep cobalt blue that didn't make it any less hot. It showed skin, a lot of it.

And all thoughts of delaying anything disappeared.

The garter belt gave her the look of a wanton, the G-string under it was an invitation to sin. The bustier she wore on top made her slight curves look bounteous.

And stopped just shy of her nipples, which stood out as hard points. Desire thudded through him. He couldn't help staring at the dark circles of her areolas. He wanted his mouth on them, he needed to be inside her, feeling her clutch hot and tight around him.

"What do you think?" Cilla asked, turning to give him the full three-hundred-and-sixty-degree view.

Rand wasn't sure coherent thought was in the program, especially when all the blood was pooled in his crotch.

She looked like a naughty schoolgirl, amused with her own daring. She looked like a temptress accustomed to making strong men weak. She looked like a woman of flesh and blood and unapologetic appetites. And all he could do was want her.

"Surely this isn't too over the top for the Annex," Cilla said, walking toward him. "All women want to walk on the wild side now and again. This is just a classier version. Feel," she invited him, and leaned closer so that he could. "Pure silk, even the lace. Everything's soft and beautiful," she said, putting her hands on his to guide them over the boned silk sides of the bustier. "And sexy," she leaned in to whisper.

He slid his fingers down over the smooth fabric,

over the silky lace, and onto the warm softness of her bare skin. She caught her breath. He felt her shiver, and for a moment she swayed. Then she drew away.

"I take it this one passes muster." She swallowed. "So that means the hot and the hotter versions work. Let's see how you do with hottest." She turned away, leaving him on the couch.

The minutes ticked by and Rand sat, waiting for the throbbing of the blood in his head and his cock to lessen. He seized the glass of water and drank, but his throat remained dry. The room suddenly felt twenty degrees warmer than it had earlier. He started to unbutton his sleeve.

"Let me help you with that," Cilla said. He looked up to see her in the archway. His first thought was that her label of "hottest" didn't really fit because she wore only a black silk kimono-style robe along with stockings and black stilettos.

She walked toward him, unbelting the robe, and only then did he realize that underneath the robe lay black silk. Barely.

His cock turned to granite.

He'd always thought that the adage that a little clothing was sexier than none was horse puckey. As far as he was concerned, the bare female body was as sensual as it got.

Time to reconsider, he thought feverishly.

The scraps of black silk were designed to frame, not provide a barrier. They didn't make even a pretense at modesty, just drew attention to themselves and the body beneath. Her breasts were the first things he noticed, outlined in a cupless bra that mostly consisted of a few strips of lace. The thong was split down the center, he saw as she walked. Desire flushed her face and darkened her eyes.

He ached to touch her.

Cilla stopped in front of him and reached out for his cuff. He leaned forward to touch her with the other hand, smoothing his palm down her silky thigh. "It's hard for me to get to these buttons," she said, and moved in to straddle him on the couch.

Her legs were warm against his as she shrugged the silk of her robe back off her shoulders. Now, she managed to unfasten the buttons and roll up first one sleeve, then the other. "That doesn't seem like enough, does it?" she murmured. "Maybe we should just get you out of this shirt altogether."

THOSE HANDS, those hands, curved around her waist as she worked to open his shirt, skimming her ribs, the fragile skin on the outside of her breasts where it was framed by mere ribbons of silk. When he touched her nipples, Cilla gasped and pressed her breasts against him, forgetting for a moment her work.

He didn't linger, though. Instead, he returned to her thighs, running over her hips before tracing back, working his way up the tender inside this time.

Cilla pulled open his shirt, tugged it out of his trousers impatiently. She wanted to be up against him. His undershirt provided only a tantalizing glimpse of the body that she knew lay beneath. She wanted more. She wanted it all.

Rand ran his hands over her forearms and up under the loose sleeves of her robe, sensitizing the skin. He started at her neck and trailed his fingertips down to where the neckline of the robe hung down her back, then forward. Cilla shivered as he traced the line of her shoulders, her collarbone, closer and closer to her breasts. She held her breath, waiting for his touch to return there.

Instead, he slipped his hands higher, around the nape of her neck and pulled her down toward him to fuse their mouths together.

And sent her spinning.

A person could go mad with desire, mad with wanting when it was stretched out so far, she thought. The taste of his lips, the brush of his tongue as they devoured each other only served to tantalize, not satisfy. With a sound of impatience, Cilla pressed against him.

Then his fingers slid up between her legs, where she was slick, wet and completely open.

Cilla cried out against his mouth. She jolted, moaned as his clever, clever fingers slipped and swirled, beckoned and tormented. They slid over the hard nub of her clit, now dipping into her deep and sudden until she bucked with the sensation, until her body came with the bursting climax that stretched out and out until she should have been limp with it.

But all she wanted was more.

"Let me," she whispered, reaching for his belt. Instead, he caught her wrists.

"No." His voice was ragged. "Not this time. I want to be in you, now." He moved to put her aside and rise.

Cilla just laughed and reached into the pocket of her robe. "You can be," she breathed, her mouth dry with desire.

He gave her a deep, hard kiss that only left her wanting, that left her hands shaking as she unzipped his pants and pulled him out.

"Let me," he ground out, taking the condom. His cock was deep, deep red and shuddering. She watched him suck in a breath through his teeth and close his eyes for a moment. When he opened his eyes they were dark pewter, his gaze was pinned to hers for an endless moment before he looked away to roll on the condom in one economical movement. He put his hands on her waist to position her, and locked eyes with her.

And in one swift motion pulled her down onto his cock.

He thrust in, so deep and so hard that she cried out with the goodness of it. For a moment, all they could do was stay motionless, linked, letting the wave of initial sensation subside. Then Cilla gripped his shoulders and began to move. Rand's hands around her waist helped set her rhythm. It wouldn't last long, she knew. They'd spent too much time building to this moment, and orgasm hovered in the hypersensitivity of her body, in the hardness of his erection.

Trembling on the edge, Cilla felt the surge, the build with each stroke. Then Rand cursed as he went past the point of no return. His cock thickened and his body clenched in orgasm.

And Cilla's body answered with its own paroxysm of pleasure.

9

HE'D ALWAYS BEEN an early riser, even when he hadn't had a lot of sleep.

Even when he'd spent the whole night turning a lover and himself inside out.

Rand surfaced to consciousness to find himself in bed, naked, with a warm, soft, slumbering Cilla wrapped around him. Reality hit home, and with a vengeance. He couldn't cuss or punch a wall. Instead, he squeezed his eyes shut and pressed his head back into the pillow.

He'd always been competitive, driven to succeed. He'd always had a plan. More often than not, he'd gone outside the normal channels in search of success, but he classed those as calculated risks that had, on the whole, paid off.

What he'd done the night before had been a risk, but not calculated in any sense of the word. What it had been, pure and simple, was a case of letting his wants get the better of his common sense.

And he'd been out of junior high far too long to be letting his gonads run his life. Or so he'd thought. Sex with Cilla had been hot the first time. Round two had pretty well blown the top of his head off. How did they both put that aside and go back to business as usual?

How did they not?

Right now, the question was what happened next. He squinted at the clock. Five-thirty in the morning, and he had an eight o'clock telecon. Well, what happened first was a shower, then a trip home for a change of clothes, then a cab to the office, arriving early enough that no one, hopefully, noticed his car had been there all night.

Figuring out a course of action made him feel marginally more in control, but not by much. He was just ignoring what really mattered, which was how they dealt with this situation. Rand knew what he wanted but he also knew it didn't make sense. He didn't have a clue what Cilla's play was going to be. It was one thing to say everything was cool beforehand. After was a whole different ball game.

More than anything, what was important was having a conversation with Cilla, figuring out their next step.

Rand squeezed his eyes shut again. Later. He'd think about that one later. For a moment, just for a moment, he allowed himself to simply close his eyes and enjoy holding her, savoring the feel of her body against his. Just to imagine for a moment how it would be if they could make it work.

And the next instant, Cilla was shaking his arm. "Rand, wake up, it's after seven."

"After what?" He looked at the clock and cursed. Adrenaline surged through him as he yanked the covers back. "I've got an eight o'clock call with Ken on the London project." He was out of bed and across the room before he realized it, feeling as if his body was still behind him, under the covers and fast asleep.

"We can work this," Cilla told him rapidly, flipping on the bathroom light. "Let's get showered and I'll drive you to your house to change. Where do you live?" She turned on the water.

"The Wilshire Corridor. Look—" he rubbed at his eyes "—I'll get a cab. Go ahead and take your time getting ready."

"What planet do you live on? It takes half an hour to get a cab in L.A., if you're lucky. I can be ready in fifteen. Come on."

She tugged him into the stream and he cursed at the still cold water. This wasn't what he'd planned. He'd planned to wake her before he left and have a talk. Or at least, plan to have a talk.

He knew, though, what they said about best-laid plans.

He had to hand it to Cilla, she was as good as her word. Most of the women he'd been involved with took an hour or more to get ready, and a rush job didn't happen much faster. Cilla, though, was a pro. She combed her hair back into the slick boy style, zipped through her makeup and slipped into a stretchy outfit that didn't require ironing—and did some very salutary things for her figure.

He was tying his shoelaces even as she finished.

"All right," she said, grabbing her handbag, "let's get you where you're going."

She was an efficient driver, aggressive enough to deal with the cutthroat morning traffic without being stupid. Still, they didn't reach his building until nearly twenty of eight. Cilla pulled up into the loading zone and shifted into neutral. "Okay, you want to make this, you've got about five minutes to change. I'll be waiting."

Rand hesitated. "I really need to take a cab in."

"There is no way you're going to get one at this hour."

And his temper got away from him. It was directed at her, at the situation they found themselves trapped in, but most of all at himself. "I know what you told me, Cilla, but I am not walking into that building with you late and with anybody who happens to be there before us noticing that my car was already in the garage."

A few seconds went by. Cilla turned off the ignition and leaned back to look at him. "Okay," she said carefully, "call it a wild stab but I'm guessing that this is about much more than being late to work."

"I could give a shit about being late to work," he snapped. "What I am concerned with is my reputation at the company, and yours. For chrissakes, we just did about the most idiotic thing we could do." He tried to ignore the little flicker of hurt that he glimpsed in her eyes.

"You weren't this bothered about it in the board meeting," she said, her voice carefully neutral.

"Oh, come on. When we slept together then we didn't know what we were doing. What was the point in being ticked? This is different. We know who we are now—and so does everybody else in the Danforth building. We should have known better." He should have known better. No matter how much she pushed, he should have been able to say no. He shouldn't have taken the chance.

And he shouldn't still ache for her now.

"Rand, relax," Cilla said, even as tension vibrated in her words. "Who's going to know?"

"What, you think no one's going to notice when we walk in and your hair's wet?"

Her chin came up at that. "No, if we're smart, I don't think they will."

"Cilla, people always see more than you expect, especially when it's you, the Danforth daughter."

"It's none of their business what I do," she retorted. "What should matter is whether I get the job done."

"And you're being naive if you think that's the way it works," he shot back. "Maybe you're a Danforth and no one's going to mess with you, but I don't have that luxury. And if you think your daddy's not going to care that I'm sleeping with his daughter then you're nuts."

And that quickly, her eyes lit in long held fury. "Don't you dare give me that crap," she hissed. "You think I've got it easy because I'm a Danforth? I've had to work twice as hard to get anywhere because of it. My father blows off everything I do. The rest of them think I'm getting a free ride, so every boss I've ever had has set the bar doubly high.

"You know how I got my position as buyer?" she demanded. "When the spot came open and I applied, they told me I wasn't seasoned enough, even though I'd been assistant buyer for four years and an intern for four years before that. Not seasoned enough," she repeated, her cheekbones stained an angry red. "So I sent in a résumé under a fake name and I got a callback the next day. They were thrilled with me. And then they found out who I really was."

That wasn't even the first time she'd pretended to be someone else to escape the Danforth legacy, he realized, and he saw the stakes were far higher than he'd ever guessed. "And now they trust you enough to give you the Annex."

She gave a bark of humorless laughter. "Give me? They didn't give me a thing, except a baby-sitter. Even they had to admit that I made sense, but what did they do? They yanked you out of Europe to watch me because my father still thinks I'm his little girl who can't get out of her own way. Dammit," her voice rose in a passionate torrent, "I got a dual business and design degree from UCLA. I got an M.B.A., with honors, from Pepperdine business school. All I want is to be given a chance to do what I know how to do. So don't tell me I'm getting an easy ride with my name. If you're scared to take a chance then fine, but don't use me as your excuse."

Hurt burned in her eyes, and betrayal, he saw. And regret swamped him. "Look, I—"

"Go upstairs and call your cab, Rand," she said icily, starting up the car. "I've got to get to work."

CILLA SAT AT HER COMPUTER, staring at the columns of inventory and sales figures and trying to make herself care. Normally, she got a charge out of reviewing the figures, analyzing the data to extract the trends, the successes, the failures. Now, she could barely make herself concentrate, as her fight with Rand kept playing over and over in her head.

How could he understand so little, have so little faith in her? All right, so maybe sleeping together wasn't the best decision in the world, but he'd been there, too. There was no reason they couldn't deal with it, no reason it had to hurt them.

Of course, that wasn't what stung. What really stung was knowing that he, too, thought she got an easy ride by being her father's daughter. If Rand, of all people, didn't understand what she was about, then how could her career at Danforth ever work? Not for the first time, she wondered about working elsewhere, but how could she translate what she knew how to do except to the competition, and every iota of her rebelled against that idea.

She pulled out a sheet of paper and began sketching garments, as she always did when she got upset about work. She sketched and dreamed about a career as a designer.

But she came back to the same answer she always did: business was what she did best and she belonged at Danforth. The thing to do was tough it out, prove herself even if she had to do it fifty times over. Eventually, she'd prevail. The Annex was one small step on that rocky path. And if Rand's words had hurt her that morning, then she needed to put them aside and move on.

How, of course, was the question. She wasn't sure what was worse, the prospect of working with him or the prospect of being without him. She supposed it underscored his point about the foolishness of getting involved with a co-worker. When things went south, it just made everything harder. You didn't always get to choose, though.

She wanted him and she wanted him a thousand miles away.

Wearily, Cilla set her drawing aside and took another look at her figures.

A knock sounded on her door. She looked up and a smile spread over her face. "Uncle Burt," she said with genuine pleasure.

He came in, comfortably padded and looking distinguished for all that. "How's my brilliant girl doing?"

"I've had more brilliant days, that's for sure," she told him ruefully, "but I'm fine, I'm fine." Burt Ruxton was like a second father to her, sometimes more like a father than her own. Just being around him was a comfort, with his perpetual kindly good humor. "Just a little stressed out over making everything work."

Ruxton sat in her client chair and shifted a little, making it creak. "Don't be. If we hadn't been sure you could do it, we'd never have given you the project."

"Really?" She couldn't help pushing. "And you didn't give it to me because I was a Danforth?"

He snorted. "Are you joking? We had people in there arguing against giving it to you for precisely that reason."

"What did you think?"

"What I always think. That you'd do us proud." He gave her a wink and Cilla was swamped with the sudden urge to weep. She fought it off but it must have shown because he frowned in concern.

"Hey, now, what's wrong?"

She shook her head. "Nothing. I'm sorry, I'm just stressed out a little."

"I see. So, would you care to keep an old man company at lunch? I came to see your father but I guess he's out."

"He had to go to the New York office for the day," Cilla told him. "Spur-of-the-moment meeting with East Coast distribution."

"That's what happens when you're the big cheese. If you're like me, you get to hang around and go to lunch with pretty girls. Come out with me," he urged. "Take a break."

She might as well, Cilla thought. It wasn't as if she was getting a thing done as it was and an hour of Uncle Burt's company would do her good. She pulled her handbag out of her desk. "You're on."

"Good. You can regale me with tales from the trenches," he told her with a roguish wink and held his arm out for her. "Right this way."

CONSIDERING HOW MANY hours he'd spent at work, he'd gotten precious little done, Rand thought as he drove home. Perhaps that was because every time he'd tried to concentrate on work, instead he'd seen the hurt flickering in Cilla's eyes. However foolish making love with her had been, it had still been his choice, and he shouldn't have taken that out on her. And while he could tell himself all he wanted to that he should have walked away, deep down he knew that what had flared between them wasn't the kind of thing you walked away from.

What was between them wasn't done, either, at least not as far as he was concerned. Maybe from her point of view it was, thanks to his heavy-handed routine that morning. If he explained, perhaps it would make a difference; at the very least, he owed her an apology.

After that, they'd see.

Without consciously thinking about it, he'd driven past his high-rise and headed toward Brentwood. It was where she would go, he thought, remembering her house. She liked to party, but a person who created a space like that wasn't the sort to look for solace in a crowd. She'd lick her wounds in solitude, until she was ready to come out.

The neighborhood looked green and manicured in the slanting light of sunset. When he knocked on Cilla's front door, he could hear faint music inside. Sarah McLachlan, unless he missed his guess. It took time for her to come to the door. When she opened it, she simply looked at him, her eyes smudged with shadow.

"Can I come in?"

Without a word, she stepped back, and he followed her. She was working at her dining-room table, sketches spread out over the surface, artists' pencils lying loose. She sat in her chair.

"New stuff?"

Cilla gave a ghost of a smile. "You asked me why I started designing. It's what I do when I get frustrated with Danforth. It's an escape."

The sketches were good, he saw. She'd obviously had training. Lingerie, again, and sexy as hell. She knew what she was doing.

As if he'd had any doubt.

"Look, I owe you an apology," he said abruptly, pulling up a chair to sit by her. "What I said this morning about you being a Danforth, that was way out of line. I know you haven't been handed anything. I see how hard you work."

With a sinking feeling, he saw her blink a few times.

Not tears, he prayed in panic. They'd just complete the job of making him feel like human scum.

"I hate the thought that people think I have it easy at Danforth because of who I am." Her voice was low, so low he almost couldn't hear it over the music at first. "I'm sorry I went off on you."

He bent over to prop his forearms on his thighs and took her hands in his. They were ice-cold. "I had it coming." He looked at her intently. "I know better than to suggest that you ride on your name. Anyone with half a brain can see that's not true."

"You didn't."

"Yes, I did. But I was pissed off."

"At me?"

He shook his head. "No, at me, for not doing what I thought I should do."

"It was my fault," she said more strongly. "I shouldn't have come on to you like that."

"That's true, you did take me against my will."

This time, the smile looked more genuine. "You were putty in my hands."

"You were right when we were outside the Pleasure Zone, it was going to happen sooner or later. My mistake was thinking I could control it."

"Don't tell me you were swept away by uncontrollable passion," she said dryly.

Hope flickered through him at her tone. And hope deserved truth, he thought, if he could just get it right. "We've got something here, and I don't have as good a handle on it as I'd like to," he said slowly, looking down at their joined hands. "This morning wasn't about the work thing. That was more of an excuse." He hesitated and looked up to meet her eyes. "I was kind of freaked out. It wasn't just being late, it was this whole thing. You, me, working together. I'm used to compartmentalizing things and I can't compartmentalize this."

Cilla swallowed. "You were right, though, sleeping together doesn't make sense. I realized it when I was trying to work today. There's too much at stake."

"You actually got work done today?" He gave a lopsided smile, concentrating on the feel of her hands in his, the reality of that connection. "I keep telling myself it's the wrong thing to do, but it doesn't seem to stick. And I can't stop feeling the way I do about you."

Her eyes seemed to grow until they dominated his vision. "So what do we do? Back away and pretend it never happened?"

He studied her. "Do you really want to do that? Can you?"

"I will if it's what you want."

"It's not," he said flatly.

"What is?"

"Taking a chance. Seeing where it goes." It was like skydiving, he thought, just leaping out without a net. "Let's try it and see what happens." He pressed her hands to his lips. "You matter to me, Cilla, and I don't want to lose sight of that. So let's just give it a run. Deal, partner?"

She leaned forward to press her lips to his. "Deal."

10

CILLA KNOCKED on the apartment door. "Airport shuttle." A pair of sparrows chased one another through the courtyard of the apartment complex, swooping among the trees and bushes before perching to quarrel bad temperedly.

The door opened to reveal Trish.

"God, what are you taking?" Cilla asked her. "You look more and more gorgeous every time I see you."

Trish just gave a bashful grin. "Oh, stop it," she muttered, but her cheeks tinted with pleasure. Her red hair tumbled down her back, loose and wild. Instead of one of her habitual sweatshirts, she wore a black jacket over a silky red camisole, managing to look classy, stylish and sexy all at once. And it would not go unnoticed by the man she was flying to meet, Cilla was certain.

"Okay, bags, purse, ticket." Cilla marked off an imaginary list.

"Bags are by the door," Trish said, pointing at her luggage. "My ticket's electronic, and I've got my purse right here." She hooked the hip-length pouch over her shoulder bandolero style.

"Birth control?"

Trish grinned. "In the bag."

"How about your man?"

"He's that way." Trish pointed east.

"Oh, yeah, that's where you're going, isn't it?"

"Assuming I don't miss my plane."

"Well, I guess we'd better get you to the airport." Cilla grabbed one of the bags.

They walked out to Cilla's car, Trish practically giddy with excitement. "You can't believe how much I am dying to see Ty."

"Ah, young love, when time goes like dog years." Of course, two weeks would be a hell of a long time to do without Rand, too, now that Cilla thought about it as they stowed the bags and got in the car. Watching Trish in love was fun just because she was so obviously new to it.

"I just can't believe any of this. Really," she said now. "I mean, Ty, flying out to Boston to be at the filming of my first screenplay, all of it. Is it real?" she asked Cilla.

"It's real. I've seen the two of you together and the man is absolutely nuts about you." Cilla grinned and headed toward the airport. "You deserve this, you have all along." She raised her voice and punched on the radio. "You should be ready to yell," she shouted, pulling onto the freeway and whooping as the wind tossed her hair around. "Come on, Trish, this time tomorrow you'll be with Ty." Cilla whooped again and this time Trish whooped with her, both of them shouting like a couple of loons as they zipped down the freeway to the airport.

The giant pillars of the light sculpture at the entrance

to LAX were glowing magenta when Cilla drove past them into the vast U of the airport. She grinned at Trish. "I hope you hadn't spent a lot of time getting your hair just so. I should have put the top up."

"Yeah, but it was worth it." Trish giggled.

"Nothing like the prospect of great sex to make a woman holler."

"Speaking of great sex, what's going on with Rand?"

"Rand?" Cilla whipped into the parking garage. "Rand is fabulous." Like a shark on the hunt, she began patrolling for an empty slot. "I just love being around him, you know? We have the best time, and the sex is— aha!" she crowed, whipping into an empty space just off of the elevators.

"And the sex is?" Trish prompted.

Cilla switched off her car. "Amazing."

"So are you seeing him this weekend?" Trish pulled out the bags.

Cilla laughed. "Sort of. I guess I'm meeting his family."

"Whoa." Trish stopped and stared at her. "This got serious in a hurry."

"It's not serious." Cilla flipped her hand in dismissal. "It's just fun."

"Yeah, right. He's taking you to meet his parents?"

"Yeah, but it's not like a meet-the-parents dinner or anything," she insisted. "We're just going to be down there and they'll be where we're going."

Trish snorted. "Cilla, even as little as I've dated, I know there's no such thing as a non-meet-the-parents meet the parents."

Sudden nerves danced in Cilla's stomach. "Trish, we've only just started seeing each other."

"Not at all," Trish countered. "You were at the desert hot springs weeks ago."

"That didn't count. Good times, though," she said thoughtfully. "Look, he was supposed to spend the day tomorrow with his brother and we didn't want to be apart."

"Dog years?" Trish asked in amusement.

Cilla grinned. "Exactly. Anyway, I'm going."

"Well, no matter what you say, the same rules hold. Wear a skirt and pearls," Trish advised, humor in her eyes. "My sister would tell you image is everything." They began walking toward the elevators.

"Um, I don't think so."

"Okay, granted I think Amber is full of it most of the time, but in this particular case, I think she's right. You never get another chance to make a first impression." They stopped in front of the brushed aluminum doors.

"Trust me, pearls and a skirt won't do it."

"Where are you going?"

"Camp Pendleton, to see his brother do a triathlon."

"Ah." Trish thought for a moment. "Camouflage shorts and pearls."

Cilla just laughed.

IN THE END, SHE DID WEAR SHORTS, along with a Tommy Hilfiger T-shirt and Skechers. Casual was the order of the day, she thought, settling her Dodgers cap more securely on her head as she got out of Rand's car.

He circled around to her.

"Sorry I was late getting over to your house this morning," Cilla said.

"Well, I guess you'll just have to make it up to me, won't you?"

"So, triathlon mania, huh?" Cilla brushed at her clothes, adjusting her shirt.

"Mmm." Without warning, Rand reached out and scooped her against him. His mouth was hot on hers, sending her pulse sprinting in excitement. An instant later, he let her loose.

Pressing her fingertips to her tingling lips, Cilla looked at him. "What was that all about?"

"I figure I'll be waiting all day to really kiss you. I thought I'd store it up."

"Good thing I wore indelible lipstick," she said.

"Good thing," he agreed.

"So who's going to be here today?" They began walking down the road from the parking lot to the staging area. The dry brown hills behind them were dotted with the dusty green of mesquite and creosote bushes.

"My little brother Jeff is doing the tri. My parents and my sisters Tina and Diane are coming to watch."

It was just a casual stop-by, she told herself. Nothing to get nervous about, at least not as long as she could restrain herself from ripping his clothes off in public. "Is that the lot of you?"

"We've got an older brother, Gary, who lives in Chicago. He couldn't be here." Rand reached out to tangle his fingers in hers and draw her closer as they walked.

"A full triathlon, that's a big deal."

Humor glinted in his eyes. "Oh, we Mitchell boys are all about endurance."

"So I've discovered."

"Actually, it's not an Iron Man, it's an Olympic-length tri. Shorter course overall, maybe three hours tops."

"What's Jeff's best time?"

"At this distance?" Rand squinted. "About two and a half hours. We'll hang out for the race, go find somewhere nice for lunch, maybe hit Las Brisas in Laguna. Then again—" he stopped and pressed a kiss on her "—maybe by that time I'll just want to take you home and have my way with you."

It sent a little spurt of excitement through her. How was it that it took so little, Cilla wondered as they resumed walking. Just hearing the warm resonance of his voice could get her paralyzed with lust.

She swallowed. Probably not a good topic to be pondering when she was just about to meet his parents.

The boat basin where the triathlon was to start was a scene of controlled chaos. Triangular plastic flags fluttered from a line in the morning breeze. Numbers marked on their shoulders and thighs in black felt pen, athletes milled about in Speedos and swim caps. The PA system squawked.

"So this is what people look like with zero body fat," Cilla murmured.

"Wait until you see my brother."

"Rand," someone shouted from one side even as he spoke.

Rand led her up to a racer standing on his own. It definitely wasn't a "meet the parents" if only one person was here, Cilla reminded herself, surprised at the relief she felt.

"Hey, bud." Rand's brother raised his hand. They went through one of those complicated guy-bonding handshakes that ended with a shoulder bump. Rand turned to her. "Cilla, this is my brother Jeff."

"Hey, Cilla. Nice to meet you."

Rand looked around at the crowd. "Where's everybody else?"

"They went over to get race T-shirts. They'll be back any minute."

Jeff had the ropy look of a long-distance athlete, and grinned back at them from behind mirrored sunglasses. He seemed energized, bouncing restlessly on the tips of his toes. Not quite the way she would be if she were looking at three hours of brutal competition.

"So how do you think you're going to do?"

Jeff struck a muscle-man pose. "I vill be ze king of the world," he said in a credible imitation of Schwarzenegger.

"Mmm, careful making fun of the governor," Cilla said.

Jeff grinned. "Top twenty would make me happy. That's what I'm shooting for."

"Don't let him kid you," said a slender, dark-haired woman who walked up behind them. "He's obsessed with finishing in the top ten. That's all we've heard about for the last hour. I'm Tina," she said to Cilla, holding out her hand. An echo of Rand hovered in her smile.

"Tina's down in San Diego," Rand told her, "going to fish."

"Oceanography at Scripps," she elaborated to Cilla, with an elbow for Rand. "But I'm still the life of the party."

"Oh, yeah, nothing like squid jokes to liven things up," Jeff said.

A slightly taller, red-haired version of Tina joined them. "This is Diane," Tina stated.

"Are you Rand's friend? Nice to meet you."

"Who let this kind of ragtag bunch in?" A lovely woman with hair more silver than brown walked up, holding hands with a sturdy-looking man. Cilla could see where the Mitchell boys had gotten their looks, a perfect melding of their mother's carved cheekbones with their father's dark coloring and ready smile.

"Cilla, these are my parents, Josephine and Vinnie. Mom, Dad, this is Cilla."

"Call me Josie," his mother said. "And don't worry if you can't remember all the names. Half the time I can't keep them straight."

"Like the other day when you told me Jeff was bringing a friend to the race?" Jeff ribbed her.

"I'm entitled to a senior moment now and again," she told him haughtily.

"Don't blame me," Vinnie said. "After the first two, I voted for just numbering you. Your mother shouted me down, though."

Cilla wasn't listening at that point. He'd told his parents he was bringing her. Just what did that mean? Polite, he was probably just being polite.

But a little warm feeling blossomed in her, even so.

Just then, the announcer started calling groups of swimmers up to prepare to start. "I'd better get up there," Jeff said. "I'm in the second wave." He collected hugs from the women in the family, shoulder punches with Rand, and a solemn handshake with Vinnie. Then, flashing a smile, he jogged down to the starting line.

"I almost entered but I didn't want to show him up." Vinnie's smile was broad.

"Well, that was noble of you," Josephine told him.

"I try," he said modestly. "You inspire me." He put his arm around her shoulders and squeezed.

Cilla blinked. She wasn't sure she'd ever seen her parents touch in public. Little enough in private, for that matter.

"Okay everyone, they're getting ready to go," Vinnie said. "Let's yell 'come on, Jeff' at the count of three."

"Come on, Jeffy," Diane objected.

"All right, Jeffy. Ready?" He counted down.

"Come on, Jeffy," they chorused. Jeff turned to toss them a quick thumbs-up before he pulled down his goggles.

The Klaxon sounded and they were off.

FOR A WHILE, they just watched the swimmers. Inevitably, though, the gentle grilling began. Rand had apparently decided to leave it up to her as to how much she wanted to say about her identity, for which she was grateful. It had a way of making people tense up and she was having too good a time for that just then.

"So, Cilla, are you from around here?" Vinnie dabbed at his mouth and laid his napkin on the table.

"Pretty much. L.A., anyway," she added.

Vinnie made a mournful face. "Five kids, and the only one of the bunch who's stayed around home is Jeff."

"La Jolla is hardly thousands of miles away," Tina told him.

"Maybe, but Gary's in Chicago and Diane's in San Francisco and Rand's been off carting around Europe."

"I'm here right now," Rand reminded him, reaching out to link hands with Cilla. "I only live an hour up the road, you know."

"This month. You're waiting to go back, I can tell."

"That's all right as long as it's a short stay." Josie's eyes gleamed. "We can go visit him, take one of those cycling tours through the south of France that I've been telling you about."

"Cycling tours?" Vinnie looked at her uneasily. "Vacations are about relaxing."

She gave a beatific smile. "Exactly. Imagine riding down a country lane in the middle of all those fields of lavender."

Vinnie didn't look convinced. "I'm an old man. I'm worried about my heart."

"Then you should be happy for the chance to get some exercise. And you're not old, you're only fifty-four."

"My children have aged me before my time," he said darkly. "Then again, their mother's kept me young." He leaned over to give her a peck.

"That's why we should go on the biking tour."

He gave her a hopeful look. "What about a driving tour?"

"What about a fifty-fifty split," she said, bargaining back. "And a four-course French meal at the end of the night."

Vinnie brightened. "Four-course meal, hmm? For you, sweetie pie, I'll suffer."

Josie's mouth curved. "I thought you might."

Cilla glanced over at Rand, who wasn't, as she expected, watching his parents.

He was watching her.

The snapping jolt of connection was enough to make her dizzy. It didn't matter that she'd just eaten; she was suddenly ravenous for him.

"Look, they're coming out of the water," Vinnie cried.

Cilla blinked. Rand gave a slow smile. "I guess we'd better get on over there," he said and caught her hand as they followed his family to the transition area.

THE TRIATHLON WAS DONE, as was the lunch to celebrate Jeff's sixth-place finish. They trailed out to the parking lot and their cars.

"We hope to see you again," Josie said warmly, holding both of Cilla's hands. Vinnie caught her up in a bear hug.

And then she and Rand were on the highway, heading home.

"Your parents are so sweet. I can't believe how easy they are together. They seem like they really care for each other."

"Sure." He looked at her. "Don't yours?"

Tolerated one another out of simple habit, more like. "They're not like your parents, that's for sure. You've got to know how rare that is."

"But your mom and dad have been together for how long, now, almost thirty years? That's got to count for something."

"I guess." Grim endurance, she supposed, or maybe

stubbornness. All she'd learned from them about relationships was what not to do. Anyway, she didn't want
to think about her parents and their constant bickering.
She wanted to hold on to the golden glow of the day. "I
really had a wonderful time today, you know," she told
him.

"Does it make me a bad person to admit that I spent
the whole last hour thinking about making love with
you?"

"So that's why you didn't say a whole lot." The
brush of his fingers made her tingle.

"I was busy planning." He ran his hand up under her
shorts and slipped his fingers under the edge of her lacy
underwear.

Cilla shivered. "I love a man who's prepared," she
breathed.

11

CILLA STOOD IN FRONT of the bathroom mirror naked, drying her hair. One of the pleasures of short hair was that it didn't take long. She bent double, running the brush and hot air through it to add volume.

And a marauding hand grabbed her behind and squeezed.

She yelped and jumped upright. "Stop that. Masher."

"Well, if you're going to stand around naked like that, you're taking your chances." Rand grinned at her impudently, deodorant in hand.

"Can't a poor helpless woman get dressed for work without some sex-crazed man coming after her?" she asked primly.

"I suppose. If she were trying to get dressed. You, however—" he swept her close and slid one hand up over her breast "—are just standing here like this because you know it drives me crazy."

"We've got to get to work," she told him, but her blow-dryer lowered to rest on the counter as her muscles weakened. The warmth of his lips trailing over the line of her shoulder blended with the brush of his fingers on her nipples. Her system stuttered. Good grief what this man could do to her. "It's after seven-thirty," she managed, even as she turned her head to kiss him.

"Mmm." He stopped abruptly and dropped his hands. "Well, I guess you're right. We should get going."

"Tease." Cilla aimed a swat at him as he stepped out of reach. "I'll teach you to get me all het up and disappear."

"You did teach me," he reminded her with a cocky grin, walking out of the bathroom into his bedroom.

She followed moments later, watching him step unapologetically naked into his closet. He had a gorgeous body, she thought, all long lines of muscle and sinew and she just admired it for a moment before turning to the bedside chair that held her overnight bag. "So why's it okay for you to walk around bareass and not me?" she challenged.

He poked his head out of the closet. "I'm walking around bareass in the privacy of my bedroom," he pointed out.

"So am I." She rummaged for her underwear and bra.

"No," he corrected, "you're running around bareass in the privacy of *my* bedroom, which pretty much makes you fair game for my animal lust."

"Animal lust, hmm?"

"Want me to demonstrate?" He slipped his arms around her and burrowed against her neck.

She made a soft sound and leaned into him. "So, what are your plans for tonight?"

"Oh, I can demonstrate now," he said indistinctly as he kissed her breasts.

"Animal," she murmured, then squealed as he tumbled her onto the bed. "You're kind of a rise-to-the-occasion kind of guy, aren't you?" she asked breathlessly, nibbling on the taut skin of his throat.

"I'm nothing but a rise-to-the-occasion kind of guy," he assured her, sliding her hand down to demonstrate. "Just let me at your occasion."

Cilla rolled in bed until she was on top of him. "I've got to take my occasion and get to work, thank you very much. You know, for some guys, the shower would have been enough."

Rand pulled her close, running his hands down her back and over her hips. "I'm what you call a motivated self-starter."

"Do tell." The stroking had her softening against him until she caught sight of the clock. She wiggled against him a little, then eeled her way off the bed.

"Only when pressed. So why were you asking about tonight?" Rand followed her and opened his bureau for a T-shirt.

"I keep forgetting to ask you. I've got to go out tonight and I thought you might want to join me."

"I always want to join you. What am I joining you for?" he asked, slipping the shirt over his head.

Cilla grinned, enjoying herself. "Oh, something I need to do."

"Why do I always get uneasy when you get vague?"

She unzipped her garment bag that hung on the back of the door. "Because you're too suspicious. It's for a good cause and it's sort of a work thing."

Rand walked back into the closet and pulled on a pale blue dress shirt. "Fun, fun, fun."

"It'll be more fun for me if you go," she wheedled as she slipped into a fifties-style halter dress in polka-dot white. She pushed up the zipper partway, then walked over to the closet door and turned her back to him. "Help me with the zipper?"

"Speaking of fun."

"Up, I meant," she said, shivering from the touch of his lips to the nape of her neck.

"You should be more specific."

"Mr. Clock says seven-forty."

Rand sighed and closed the zipper. "So this thing tonight is probably boring and it's for work, which means keeping my distance."

"Not necessarily," she pointed out, turning to button his shirt. "We'll be representing Danforth and the Annex, so we can at least sit together. Trust me, you'll love it," she assured him. He smelled clean and just a little spicy. It was too short a distance between them for her to resist leaning in for a kiss. Such a shame it was a weekday, she thought, luxuriating for a moment in the softness of his mouth.

Work, she remembered, and pushed away.

"I'll love it, huh?" Rand said, and stole one last peck before turning back to dressing. "We never established just what, exactly, it is."

"The Video Style Awards and Charity Auction. We're cosponsors."

He rolled his eyes and turned to pull a pair of trousers off their hanger.

"You really are quite the clotheshorse," Cilla observed, peeking past him into his packed closet.

"Looking good paves the route to success." He

tucked in his shirt and buttoned up his trousers. "So can our marketing budget afford the sponsorship?"

"We can't afford not to." To her, it was as simple as that.

"That's not what I asked," he said, a slight edge to his voice.

"Danforth has covered half of it. We had a last minute chance to pick up some of it for the Annex, so I jumped on it. All the major fashion magazines will carry stories on it, and maybe *Entertainment* or the *Times*."

Rand threaded a belt through the loops in his trousers and snugged it up. "I don't remember hearing about this."

"It just came up. Forth's gets the TV spots, but we can work the event for the Annex."

"TV?"

She shrugged lightly. "You're running with a fast crowd now."

"I'll say. Next time you make a decision like this, though, let's talk it over first. We don't have much of a budget and we both need to be in on the numbers, at least for a while."

"Sure. So will you be my date?"

He hung a tie around his neck and walked over in front of his mirror. "Gee, I don't know. I could be sitting here by myself with a beer watching the game, or I could be out in public with you in one of those sexy little numbers." He considered as he began wrapping the tie into a knot. "Tough choice, but I think I have to go with the game."

Cilla launched herself at him, tipping him back on the bed. "Say uncle," she demanded, kissing him. "Say it."

He rolled over until she was underneath him on the bed. "Uncle," he murmured. "And just how long does this charity event last?"

Cilla sighed. "Dinner, then the auction. After that, we just have to sit in the dark and clap. We could probably even leave after the break."

He pulled her close. "I think that's a must," he murmured.

RAND WALKED THROUGH the back door of the Annex, threading his way through the maze of boxes in the stockroom to emerge by the changing rooms. Paige had already worked her magic in this area, the doors of the cubicles bold splashes of color amid black and white. The look was emerging, and he liked it.

In the main part of the store, the fixtures were going up. A radio played faintly in the background over the sound of an electric drill. Cilla stood talking with Paige, watching the contractors hang wallpaper.

It never failed, the buzz he got from seeing her. It was like going to the ice-cream store when he was a kid: the anticipation of a sweet treat, the excitement of not knowing the flavor of the day, and the sheer pleasure of the moment he placed a bite on his tongue and let the rich sweetness flow through him.

Cilla's face lit up as she caught sight of him.

"Well, if it isn't the Boy Wonder himself," she said as he approached.

"In the flesh," he agreed. "Hi, Paige."

"Hi, Rand."

"The place looks good. We going to be on schedule for the opening?"

"We should be." She consulted her clipboard. "The

holdup was the wallpaper, but once you guys gave the okay to pay for a separate production run at the factory, we were all set."

"Really?" He looked at Cilla. In his personal life, he might like surprises. In his professional life, almost never—and this was the second one that day. He bit back the urge to demand information, though. Maybe it wasn't what it sounded like. Later, he promised himself. They'd deal with it in private.

"The couches came in." Paige walked them over to the display windows, now screened off from the outside world with heavy brown paper. "It's hard to see under all the plastic, but they're fabulous."

They looked familiar to him. "Isn't that a Barcelona chaise?"

Paige looked impressed. "You've got a good eye."

"Not really. I lived over in Italy for a while and did some furniture shopping." And a real Barcelona was pretty spendy, he recalled.

"Cilla and I went to the Pacific Design Center and picked these out." She smoothed a hand over the back of the chaise. "Quality shows."

And quality costs. "It looks great, Paige. Will you excuse us a minute?"

HE TIPPED HIS HEAD toward the back and started walking, expecting her to follow him like an unruly child about to be disciplined, Cilla thought with a surge of temper. Well, she wasn't going to explain herself. She was in charge of the redecoration and the decisions were hers to make.

Rand shut the stockroom door behind them and

turned to face her. "How much are we over budget, Cilla?"

She had to hand it to him, he didn't waste time. "Not much. You get overage on any project like this."

"Not this kind of overage."

"What do you mean?" And how did he know?

"We're looking at an expedited delivery fee for the wall covering, and I know those chaises cost a bundle because I was looking at them myself when I lived in Milan. I make six figures and I couldn't justify them."

"You were looking at retail price. Paige gets them at trade."

"How much, Cilla?"

She capitulated. "We're about twenty percent over."

His eyes widened a fraction, and for the first time she felt a little spurt of alarm. "The *project* is twenty percent over?"

"No." She moistened her lips. "The redecoration."

She saw the temper flare. "Cilla, we had a budget for a reason."

"All projects have overruns, Rand. This one was no exception."

"We're facing some very aggressive profit goals, here. It'll be a miracle if we make those numbers, even if we do stay on budget, but at least we've got a fighting chance."

"Look, higher profits means higher revenues, and that means getting the traffic in here," she said hotly. "The store has to look right. If it even hints at bargain hunting, we won't get the customers we need."

"You think a couple of couches are going to do it?"

He made her feel as if she was being called to account by a parent or a boss and she bridled. "It's not just the couch, Rand. It's the overall look. And the chaises weren't what blew the budget. No one thing was. It was piecemeal, and they were the right choices to make."

"Individually, maybe, but a smart project manager makes trade-offs. You put the money out in some places and hold back in others. We could have worked something out." He raked his hair back off his forehead with one hand. "You should have asked me."

"I didn't know I needed your permission for everything," she flared.

"You don't need my permission." He stepped up to her. "You need my agreement. We're partners, remember?"

It was about more than irritation over the project, she realized. It was about being let down, being kept out of the loop. And that quickly, her anger evaporated.

Cilla shook her head. "I'm sorry. I just didn't think about it. It was five hundred here, a grand there. It didn't seem like that much money." She met his eyes. "I figured it would come out in the wash. I was wrong." And it was all so obvious to her now that she should have kept him informed.

"It's okay." Rand took a deep breath and relaxed his shoulders. "It's okay," he said again. "We're just figuring out how this all works."

"Do you want me to cover it? I can," she offered.

He gave a crooked smile. "If we miss our marks because of that, we've got bigger problems than just a decorating overrun. Just talk to me next time, okay? Are we a team on this?" He stared at her.

Cilla let out a breath. "We are." She wanted to touch

him, to reassure herself that everything was right between them. Now was not the time, though.

Rand leaned in to press a kiss on her forehead. "It's okay. We're okay," he said softly, and stepped back. "Now why don't you show me what's new?"

CILLA HAD THE TOYS laid out in a discreet room tucked away in the back.

"Christmastime for good little girls," Rand said dryly.

"And boys." She slanted him a look. "It's not all about us, you know."

"That's when it's most fun, though."

The look in his eyes gave her a little shiver in the pit of her stomach.

He picked up a bottle at random. "So, you've got the garden-variety lotions and oils."

"Something to be said for lotions and oils," Cilla reminded him.

"And how." His voice was fervent.

She'd set out a few of the items on the display area Paige had designed. It was an alcove set back from the rest of the store, made to look like a boudoir, with a dressing table, a nightstand and a slice of bed showing. Cilla D. lingerie hung from the closet bar and showed in the open drawers of a fixture similar to a bureau. The bottles and toys sat on the bedside table.

Rand poked at a pale pink oblong plastic egg that sat next to a vibrator. "What's this, defective merchandise?" he asked, tossing the egg in his hand.

Cilla didn't say anything, just picked up a small gadget that looked like a garage-door opener with a butterfly emblazoned on it.

And Rand jumped as the egg buzzed in his hand.

"Our future top seller." She tossed the remote control to him.

"For the girl who has everything." He set the egg down on the dresser.

"Something like that, yes."

Rand pressed the switch and the egg jumped and began to rattle on the table. He caught it before it rolled off. "This has some seriously interesting possibilities," he told her.

"Ain't modern technology wonderful?"

"Not nearly as good as the old-fashioned way." He checked his watch. "Speaking of which, it's after five. Maybe we should call it a day. Want to meet at your house or mine?"

"Mine. I've got to change."

"I'll stop by the office then and pick you up at what, seven?"

"I'm going to head out right now. I've just got to stop and pick up a couple things and I'll go right home. Why don't you meet me at six?"

"Sure. I can help you get undressed."

IN THE END, RAND SAT on her front step until six-thirty, another chunk of time after a long, frustrating day of look-but-don't-touch. The wanting was a physical throb within him. When he saw her, it rose to an ache, and they were no sooner in the door than he caught her to him. In the aftermath of their argument, he'd wanted only to hold her. He hadn't been able to do that then, but he could now, he thought, luxuriating in the feel of her springy body against him. "So where is it that we have to go again?" he murmured against her neck.

"Mmm. The charity auction."

"Can't we just send them a check?"

"We already have, silly. What we're going to do tonight is get the payoff." She pressed a kiss on him. "Now let me loose, I have to change."

"We can be late," he told her, his fingers searching out her zipper.

Cilla twisted away from him. "We're already late."

"We can be later."

"I'll miss the press people I want to see," she explained. For just a moment, she took him deep with lips and teeth and tongue, pressing her mouth to his. Then she broke the kiss, resting her forehead against his chin, breathing hard. "I don't want to do this now but I have to, especially after the conversation we had today."

Rand sighed. "All right, I'll suffer."

"You're so understanding. Do you need to change?"

He looked down at his suit. "What, Armani isn't good enough?"

"Good point." For a moment, she just stared at him. "You look wonderful."

"I look even better naked."

Cilla just laughed. Rand followed her to her bedroom and leaned against the wall to watch her change. He'd always loved this part, the concentration and pleasure that women brought to dressing to go out. Guys just grabbed clothes and dressed. For women, it was like a military operation. The choice of outfit was just a start, the selection of accessories critical. The hairstyling alone was a delicate minuet. And there was that special something in the way a woman held herself when she was perfumed and primped and looking her best.

Cilla opened up her closet and studied the clothing inside for a moment, then pulled out a hanger. On it was a silky robe, deep blue with a copper edging that gave it a vaguely Roman look. Cilla slipped into it and clasped it at the waist with a wide copper belt. Rand blinked. "Is that for inside or outside," he asked.

Cilla just laughed and ducked into her bathroom, closing the door. When she came out, she'd added copper links at her earlobes and a copper cuff around her wrist. The cosmetics weren't obvious but her mouth was lush and kissable, her eyes more vivid.

She was beautiful.

He finally got his jaw to move. "Do we really have to go?"

Cilla kissed him lightly. "Duty calls." Then she laughed. "Don't look so down. We'll be back in two hours, I swear."

"It's the two hours I'm worried about."

They walked out into the living room and Cilla transferred her wallet and keys into a copper envelope purse she carried. She opened the front door and looked back at Rand. "Maybe this will keep you entertained in the meantime." She walked outside.

Rand looked to see what she'd given him and grinned.

It was a remote control with a butterfly.

12

THE ENTRANCE to the Video Style Awards and Charity Auction was padded with a red carpet. Camera flashes popped as fashion mavens from Hollywood and the music industry alike walked in. It was interesting, Cilla mused, how intermingled style and entertainment had become. Magazines, cosmetics and clothing lines chose actresses for their models even as models crossed over into acting.

As far as Cilla was concerned, it didn't matter where their loyalties lay. She wanted the entertainment A list at the Annex. The resultant buzz would give the store the exposure it needed. She could see it now—Buzz Builders Like Megan Barnes Dip Into The Annex For Cilla D. And The Latest Designers. It would only take a couple of stories like that for the spin to become self-perpetuating.

It helped that the magazine editors were old friends that she'd grown to know over the years at runway shows in New York, Tokyo, Milan, Paris. The casual references she'd made at the spring shows bore fruit now in equally casual conversations about the progress of Cilla D. and its launch. Yes, they'd be able to see the line in a matter of days; yes, she was setting up a show the following month at the Annex. Oh, hadn't they heard about the Annex? It was the latest and greatest from Danforth, opening in days, and the exclusive source for Cilla D.

She laughed and joked and introduced Rand, who charmed them all. By the end of it she'd received demands for invitations to the grand opening. By the time cocktails were over, she'd managed to let it drop to a number of actresses and performers. All in all, a good night's work, she told herself as the lights dimmed slightly for the auction and the audience focused on the podium.

"And have we done our duty?" Rand asked softly.

Cilla nodded. "You've been very good."

"I don't have to actually buy anything, do I?"

"You can just sit here and look pretty." She patted his thigh.

A truly awful outfit went up on the block, a silvery butterfly-sleeved fright that looked as if it was made from the foil off a package of Jiffy Pop.

"Now, that comes under the heading of 'wouldn't be caught dead in it,'" she murmured.

Rand chuckled and the sound of it hummed in her bones. "Don't be so harsh. I think it's kind of sexy."

"Then you buy it."

The auctioneer started into his singsong. "Okay, bidding starts out at five thousand dollars, am I bid five thousand, five thousand."

And abruptly, a buzz went through her, starting between her legs and jolting her down to her toes. Her hand flew up.

"Five thousand from the young lady in blue," the auctioneer said instantly.

Cilla's eyes widened. "I didn't..." she protested, but the auctioneer was already back into his singsong chant.

"Five thousand, five thousand, we've got a five thousand dollar bid, ladies and gentlemen. This is an original design by Koizumi in silver sequins. It retails at more than twenty thousand dollars. Come on, folks, this is to benefit the L.A. Charities Foundation and it'll look good on the red carpet. Bring out your checkbooks."

Cilla leaned over to Rand. "I'd better not win this," she muttered. It was improbable, but in the hustle of working the reception, she'd forgotten the egg, and perhaps Rand had, too.

He'd remembered now, though.

Under the tablecloth, his hand settled on her thigh. "It's for a good cause," he said, and buzzed her again.

This time, the vibration sent a shudder of awareness through her. When it stopped, her nerve endings shimmered with sensation.

It left her wanting.

Rand shifted his hand on her thigh, his fingers trailing down along the inside. When the vibration came again she felt the little curl of tension and her lips parted.

Rand just looked at her and smiled.

The auctioneer went off to another prize, having coaxed the bidding on the silver dress up to well over retail. Cilla didn't care. Her attention was occupied elsewhere.

Rand just leaned back in his chair, one hand on her leg, the other in his pocket. He was maddeningly inconsistent, sometimes teasing her with brief pulses that set all her nerve endings on end, other times turning up the intensity so high that she fought to keep from shuddering. Sometimes it was only enough to make her wiggle a bit.

She could feel herself getting wet.

Cilla shifted in her seat. She caught her breath and tensed. When she moved just right, the pulsation felt as if it was running through her body to her clit. And the wanting thrummed through her.

It wasn't a game anymore. The arousal was deep and strong. She ached to have Rand inside her. She stirred again.

"What's the matter, got ants in your pants?" Rand gave her a devilish look.

"Something like that."

The vibration vanished and she felt a flare of disappointment. Of need. Her awareness was complete. The stimulation might have awoken her nerve endings, but it wasn't enough. She had to be touched, now. Warm flesh and muscle. Hands on her breasts. A hot mouth on hers, a hard cock driving into her, she needed it. She craved it. The last thing she wanted was to be sitting in this room of Hollywood and musical talent, decorously watching the auction.

Rand's fingers began stroking up the tender skin of her inner thigh.

"Can I get you coffee, cappuccino, an after-dinner drink?" It was the waiter, standing over her.

"Yes, please. I'd like…" Cilla's voice wavered as Rand buzzed her. "Ice water, please," she said more firmly, resisting the urge to move against the vibration, against Rand's hand.

"And you, sir?"

"I don't think so," Rand answered. "I'll be leaving soon."

Cilla's entire being was focused now on the throbbing between her thighs, and a shudder of true arousal passed through her.

Rand just looked at her, his eyes hot and dark. In that moment, she didn't care about work, about Danforth, about the Annex, about anything but him.

And she rose.

NEED BOUNCED THROUGH Cilla in time with the pulsing of the vibrator, as she and Rand waited for the car. He had the vibrator throbbing on low. It made her knees weak and she clutched his arm.

"I want you now," she murmured to him.

His response was to turn up the vibrator until she nearly whimpered. "Patience. In the meantime, you can enjoy it."

"You're driving me crazy."

The valet pulled up in the car and Rand handed her into it. Sitting in the car seat focused the throb on her clit and she made a small sound.

"Ready to go?" Rand asked as he put the car in gear.

Her response was a moan.

Rand's right hand traced its way up her thigh as he drove, sliding up the aquamarine silk to reach trembling flesh. "Where are we going?" he asked.

"Wherever's closer." Brentwood and the Wilshire Corridor seemed miles away. She wasn't sure she could wait that long. "They're both too far," she said raggedly.

"You're so wet," he murmured, sliding his fingers up between her slick folds and then he froze. "I have an idea." He whipped the car into a quick turn, then swung around into a back alley.

And Cilla knew where they were.

Getting inside the Annex took only a moment. With shaking fingers, Cilla punched the necessary code into the security keypad to disable the alarm. Then Rand pressed her against the wall and put his mouth to hers, whirling her away into a hot urgency. Sensation swamped her until it was difficult to think. After existing in a state of suspended desire, she was finally free to feel what she craved. His hands roved over her body. He fumbled with the clasp of his belt, but she stilled his hands.

"Not here. Wait."

She knew where she wanted to go. Forget about vertical quickies. She wanted him in her hard and deep, wanted to feel his weight as he drove himself into her.

The emergency lights cast a dim glow as Cilla moved to the front of the store, catching Rand's hand to draw him with her.

To the display windows.

Light from the street lamps shone through the layers of brown paper that covered the windows, giving the space an almost luminous glow, highlighting the chaise that sat there. Cilla kicked off her shoes. Stepping up into the window, she stripped the plastic impatiently.

And sank back onto the soft, red leather.

Could a person explode from wanting, she wondered, staring back at Rand, watching him watch her as he tossed aside his jacket, his tie, his shoes. Then in the blink of an eye, he was beside her.

The first touch of his hand had her exhaling sharply as his fingers curved over her breast. He kept the thin barrier of silk in the way, letting her feel him and yet not feel him. His taste was temptation, and as his mouth trailed down from her mouth, over her jaw, and down into her neckline, she shivered.

She felt a surge of impatience and reached for his shirt, wanting his bare skin against hers. But he stilled her hands. "You wanted to wait, we wait." He unfastened her belt and spread open the robe to reveal only her thigh-high hose and the skimpy bit of lace she'd chosen to torment him with.

And he made a helpless sound.

With the fingers of his free hand, Rand traced the line of her breasts, stroking over them, brushing the nipples as they hardened. She heard him catch his breath. Then her own shuddered out as he squeezed her nipples, sending a rush of sensation through her— whether pleasure or pain, she couldn't say, didn't care. For an instant, it was enough to be lying back in the darkened store, nearly naked, feeling his touch.

Cilla arched back as he leaned over and rubbed the beginnings of his beard against her nipples in little slicing bolts that alternated with the wet warmth of his tongue. The scrape of teeth, the quick suction, the softness of his lips, it all blended in a kaleidoscope of feeling.

Then he straightened and stripped off his shirt impatiently, his chest and arms the color of burnished bronze in the dim glow. When he dropped his trousers, she could see his hard-on curving up from his body.

Desire arrowed into her.

Eyes locked to his, Cilla reached down to touch herself where she was slick, pulling out the vibrating egg.

"I don't think we need this anymore."

"On the contrary." Rand took it from her. "We're just getting started." His eyes gleamed. "You should never sell a product unless you've fully tested it."

With the vibrator gone, Cilla craved his touch. Instead, he made her wait longer.

He bent again to her breasts, licking her nipples. Then the shudder of the vibrator replaced the heat of his mouth. Cilla gave a choking laugh as the throb raced through the sensitive flesh. When he slipped his free hand down between her thighs, all laughter disappeared in a moan.

Rand groaned in tandem with her as his finger slid into the wetness between her legs. "You have no idea what it does to me when you're like this."

"I think I do," Cilla murmured, reaching out to wrap her fingers around his hard cock. "It's the same way I feel when I feel you hard." The power of her tangible attraction for him intoxicated her. "I want you inside me."

"Not yet."

He moved the egg down her body, letting the vibrations spread through her as it came nearer and nearer to her thighs. When he slid it close, though, he didn't touch her where she ached for it. Instead, he stroked it along the sensitive folds of her labia, making her writhe. He dipped it into her, finding the spot where the pulsations seemed to spread out through her entire body. And then, only then did he slide it up to the rigid bud of her clitoris.

The shadows of pedestrians strobed over the brown paper as they walked by.

Cilla stifled a cry.

Eyes intent, Rand watched her, one of his hands doing mind-bending things to her breast, the other rubbing the vibrator over her clit, rhythmically, steadily, until she was ready to scream with it. It wasn't like finding arousal with the touch of a hand or a mouth or a cock. There was no meandering journey, no progress up through level after level. The intensity flung her up and over into orgasm almost before she realized it, racking her body with shudders, dragging a helpless gasp from her.

Rand moved to slide on top of her but Cilla put a hand against his chest even as she felt the aftershocks. "Not yet. I don't think we're done testing."

"Really?"

She swore she could hear him grind his teeth. She pressed him down on the chaise. "Oh, yes. Now it's your turn to wait."

Dipping into the wetness between her legs, she spread it over Rand's hard cock, feeling him jolt against her fingers. She stroked him, rubbing the spot where she knew he was most sensitive.

And then she switched on the egg.

Slowly, slowly, Cilla stroked the vibrator up the length of his shaft where it lay hard against his belly. Rand's breath hissed in. Precome seeped out of the tip of his cock. She ran the rounded end of the egg through the slippery fluid, then stroked it along his cock, watching the shaft and glans harden and redden, watching the veins rise. Because she couldn't resist the temptation, she leaned in to lick him, then stroked him with the vibrator. Watching his reaction, she alternated between the two, licking then rubbing, licking then rubbing. He groaned and his fingers tightened on her shoulders.

Cilla moved to lie next to him on the chaise, turned on her side so that she could watch herself running the vibrator up and down until his erection pulsed against it. "Now," he commanded, shifting to press her flat on her back. The egg clattered to the floor as he slid between her legs. She felt a thrill of anticipation. And then he was inside her.

Fast and deep, the first thrust took her breath away. Rand stroked into her, rhythmic and hard, staring into her eyes. She saw his jaw clench with the effort at control even as she wrapped her arms and legs around him to pull him closer, deeper as he plunged in over and over again.

When her orgasm hit, it was more powerful than anything a mechanical toy might have brought, the heat and texture of the human touch sending her arching and shuddering against him. And the feel of his cock pulsing within her as he spilled himself, was one more wave of ecstasy.

13

IT WAS A BIG JOB, opening a store, Cilla thought wearily as she knelt down and used a box cutter to slice through the plastic binding tape around a carton of clothing. The merchandise had arrived, the ads and press releases had gone out—tomorrow was the day.

And all they had to do was get the fixtures in place and a store's worth of stock displayed or folded and put on the shelves, and the floors vacuumed and the mirrors cleaned. That wouldn't have been such a daunting task if it hadn't been for the fact that the mirrors were still being hung and portions of the tile floor were still drying.

Theoretically, they had staffers, including management, in place to do it all, but Cilla hadn't been able to stay away that morning. She needed to be there to see the progress, she needed to pitch in and be a part of it.

Which was just as well, given that Murphy and his law, as usual, had reigned supreme. Paige had never missed a deadline, but she hadn't reckoned with the vagaries of import-export. The Italian flooring had gotten held up in customs and not released until the night before. It was the next best thing to robbery, but Cilla paid the tilers enough to lay it overnight. Until the tile was put down, it couldn't dry, until it dried fixtures couldn't go into place, and until the fixtures were in place, nothing could be hung. They hadn't even gotten started until the end of the day.

No sooner had they started than one of the clerks kicked a two bar fixture, and meanwhile, a crucial shipment of clothes had failed to show up and, given that it was currently after seven at night, it was unlikely to do so.

Her and her big ideas about wanting to get the store open two weeks after their first meeting. What would one more week have hurt? But no, she wanted to get every bit of revenue during the trial period they could, and that was why they were completely under the gun.

Stay calm, Cilla told herself. She was simultaneously exhausted and amped out of her mind with stress. In a perfect world, she'd be savoring every moment of watching the store come together. Instead, she felt as if she were watching a slow-motion train wreck.

Maybe she could steal a few moments to do a little yoga in the back room, she thought. Then she remembered the condition of the back room and snorted. Not a chance. She'd be better off imagining herself doing the triangle pose and the downward dog while she hung up stock, instead.

"Having a good time?" Rand walked by carrying an armload of Prada dresses to the front.

"Deliriously." Rand was the only bright spot in the proceedings, but her mood elevation didn't last much after he passed. The thing to do was to focus on getting tasks done one after another. Eventually, it would all be finished.

Rand was back. "You okay?"

"What did you do with those three-thousand-dollar dresses?"

"Set them down on one of the chaises," he said briefly. "They're fine. You're the one I'm concerned about." He crouched down beside her and touched a hand to her cheek. "You look beat."

"I'm okay." What she wanted to do more than anything just then was hold on to him, just for a moment, to hear him say it would all be okay. But public displays of affection at work were frowned upon. That didn't stop her from wanting them. Instead, she settled for brushing the hair off his forehead. She knew that, strictly speaking, that wasn't allowed, either, but there was only so much a woman could stand, after all. "I'm just a little stressed over getting everything done."

"Relax."

"Relax? We open tomorrow at 10:00 a.m. How is all of this going to get done?"

"We've got five of us laying out stock, the contractors are almost finished putting the wall fixtures in place, and the last mirror just went up. We'll have this in shape in about two hours. Anything that doesn't get done tonight, Charla can do tomorrow."

"Two hours won't be enough," Cilla muttered.

Rand took a quick glance around and leaned in for a quick kiss, hidden by the clothing hanging around them. "It'll have to be, because at 10:00 p.m., I'm taking you home to dinner and to bed." He stood. "Now get to work."

HOURS LATER, RAND WAS flopped in bed, propped up against pillows. Cilla lay against him, relaxed and breathing deeply. He couldn't quite tell whether she was asleep or not, so he tried not to move.

The shades of the darkened room were pulled to show the full band of windows, which looked out toward the serrated bulk of the Hollywood Hills. He couldn't say he liked the apartment any better than he had when he'd moved in, but he was definitely hooked on the view.

He'd been right about the fact that it would all get done. Done, though, had been closer to 1:00 a.m. than ten. The usual brutal calculus of exhaustion had held, and the more fatigued they'd gotten, the slower it all had gone. Cilla, though, had been driven by nervous energy. She'd pushed them all the extra bit, humored, heckled, cajoled, whatever it took to get things done. She'd worked as hard as any of them, harder, even. And as though bewitched, the staff knocked themselves out for her.

And now she was out like a light, he thought, kissing the top of her head. In all too short a time she'd become necessary to him. He couldn't let himself think about it right now, not while everything was in flux. Take a risk, she'd invited him, and he had, but he'd thought it was a professional risk.

He'd never expected it to be personal.

Cilla sighed against him, then jolted and came awake. Rand stayed quiet but finally she stirred and lifted her head. "Hey." He tightened his arms around her. "Bad dream?"

"Not really." She moved to kiss him. "Dumb. You know the kind—you're walking along a curb and you step off and hit the ground too hard and presto, you're jerking awake." She leaned back against him and sighed.

"Nervous about the opening?"

She rolled her eyes. "You even have to ask?"

"I did my best to help you work off your tension," he pointed out, sliding his hand over her flat belly.

"And it worked, for about five minutes, anyway," she said ruefully. In the dark, she was just a soft voice that matched her soft skin.

"I'd be happy to take another stab at it," he offered.

"So to speak."

He chuckled. "I'm willing to sacrifice for the cause."

"If anyone could have done it, you did," she said, nestling against him.

"Then stop worrying, already."

"How?" Her voice was leaden with exhaustion. "I keep starting to fall asleep and then I think of one more thing that we've forgotten."

"If we have, it's not the end of the earth. Nothing's perfect. Shoot, the day Disneyland opened, they hardly had a single drinking fountain that worked. We're opening a boutique, not an amusement park. It doesn't have to be flawless tomorrow."

"What if my father or some of the board members show?"

"What if they do? They've been in business a long time. They know things take time." He understood her stress because he felt it, too, but he would only let it dog him so far.

Cilla sighed. "You have no idea how much I want this to be a success."

He stroked his fingertips over her cheek. "With two such brilliant minds on board, how could it not?"

She was silent for a long moment. "I just can't stop

worrying," she said, finally, in a small voice. "I'm afraid if it doesn't work it'll reflect badly on you. I don't want that to happen. And I don't want my dad to regret that he gave me the chance."

Rand felt her shake just a little and realized she was crying. "Hey," he said softly.

"I'm sorry. I know guys hate it when women cry."

"Don't worry about that," he soothed. "Where's this coming from? It's going to be fine, you know that."

"I want him to be proud of me."

And this, finally, was the root of it. He'd known it was there, he'd heard her speak of it.

He'd had no idea how deep it really went.

Rand stroked her arms. "Why wouldn't he be proud of you? Look at all you've accomplished. Of course he's proud of you. You can hear it in his voice."

She took a deep breath and let it out slowly. "There's proud of being and there's proud of doing."

"You don't think he's proud of both?"

"I don't think he thinks there's anything to be proud of, at least not in the doing part. I know he loves me, he just doesn't think much past that."

"I think you're underestimating him."

"I don't." She sat up, wrapping her arms around her knees. "I've watched him and my mom over the years. I know he doesn't respect her. I don't know if he even loves her."

"Marriages change over time," he offered helplessly.

"I watched your parents the other weekend. They're amazing. You can see how much they genuinely like and respect one another."

"My parents are kind of freaks that way," he said. It

was something he'd never seen in another couple. It was something he'd always hoped to find one day. "Your parents' relationship isn't necessarily wrong, it's just that you can't understand it from the outside."

"I don't know if it's always been that way or not." She moved her shoulders. "Maybe it was. Somewhere along the line, I realized he treated her like he treated me."

"How's that?"

"The same way you'd treat a pet." Her voice was bleak. "Indulgent, but never really listening. Never really respecting anything she did, never giving her a say in anything. Even the times he asked her opinion, you could tell he'd already decided what to do. They haven't slept together in the same bedroom for years."

She was silent for a minute. Rand reached out and ran his hand up and down her back, not saying anything.

"I want him to see. I want more from him than fatherly love. I want his respect." She turned to look at Rand over her shoulder, her eyes sad and vulnerable in the faint reflection of the city lights, and for a moment his heart stuttered.

And in that moment, he fell.

THE SUN ROSE PINKISH-GOLD into the morning sky and Cilla's mood rose with it. She'd tossed and turned all night, but each time she'd woken, Rand had been there, arms around her, keeping the worst of her demons at bay. Now, optimism filled her even as the light filled the room. The opening would be a success. How could it fail to be?

She rolled over and kissed Rand awake. "Get up, sleepyhead, I'll take you out to breakfast. What do you want to eat?"

"You." His eyes flashed open and he trapped her, giggling, against the sheets. Then her laughter turned to gulping gasps and time became irrelevant.

It was a fine way to start the day, she thought later as they did the final tidying at the Annex. The important couture shipment *had* arrived. Paige roamed the store, restlessly checking and rechecking the details. The manager for the Annex, Charla Saunders, supervised the opening of the registers.

In less than an hour, they'd unlock the doors and see who came.

Nerves bubbled in Cilla's stomach. She stood with Rand at the front of the store. "So what do you think?"

He glanced over his shoulder. "I like the chaises," he said blandly.

Cilla suppressed a smile. "Don't they give the right ambience to the place? It was money well spent."

"And how. The place looks great," he replied, turning back to survey the sleek styling that put the focus on the clothes but still had a look of its own.

"I think we did good," she murmured and hooked a hand over his shoulder without thinking as they looked out over the room. She glanced at her watch. "We should get the paper down off the windows."

Cilla kicked her heels off and climbed up on the platform of the window display. The red chaise was surrounded by beautiful clothing. They'd skipped mannequins, electing to go with garments draped over metal fixtures. It would be eye-catching, stylish and, she hoped, different.

"Okay, last minute pep talk. How much of a success will it be?" she asked Rand as he moved into the far corner of the window and began pulling loose the tape that held the paper in place.

"Stellar. Staggering. Getting cold feet?"

"Just a little chilly."

"Maybe you should put your shoes back on." He winked at her and started rolling the paper back off the window, moving toward her as he pulled it loose. "The room might be chilly, but I don't think the market's going to be. I think we're going to be okay once we get—"

"Rand."

Cilla's voice was low and shocked.

His gaze shot to her, but she was staring, white-faced at something behind him. He turned, and where they'd torn off the paper, he could see the knots of people waiting outside.

Waiting for them to open. He felt a spurt of triumph.

And the smile spread over Cilla's face like sunlight.

ONE OF THE WONDERFUL THINGS about living in L.A., Cilla thought, was that you could get just about any kind of food brought to your door, at just about any hour. It was after 10:00 p.m. and the two of them sat in her living room, eating Thai food directly from the cardboard containers.

It had been the most extraordinary day. Cilla forked up some pad thai, still giddy with success. "I remember three weeks ago standing in Diavala and thinking how much I wished the Annex could be like that."

"Looks like you got your wish," Rand said lazily, reaching for the green curry. "I think we've got a winner."

"So we've conquered the world. What do we do now?"

"First things first, make our six-month numbers." He took a bite of curry. "Which I'm thinking we've got a good chance of doing, considering we pulled in our full-week bogey today." His jaw was blued with the day's growth of beard. With his hair a tousled mess, he just gave her the urge to tumble him into bed.

"You're so sexy when you talk salesspeak." Cilla leaned over and gave him a hard kiss. When she lifted her head, her tongue was buzzing from his curry. "Not only that," she said, grabbing her beer, "you're hot."

"Don't let it get around. I restrict my services to a very limited clientele."

"Lucky me." To cool the burn, she reached for a skewer of chicken satay. "So how cool would it be if we beat our numbers? The sky would be the limit, then."

"Maybe not quite that, but we'd certainly get people's attention."

"Make one proposal work and they're a hell of a lot more likely to listen to the next one." She dipped the chicken in peanut sauce and took a bite, her mind already vaulting ahead with plans.

Rand considered. "It wouldn't hurt to have a strategy in place if things go our way."

"Not an expansion."

Rand shook his head. "No. That's not how you make the profits. The way you pull ahead isn't by a ten or twenty percent increase, it's jumping by a factor of two, or three, or five."

"Open up new stores," she said slowly.

"Exactly. Find the market and the profits will follow." He set down the carton of curry, warming to his subject. "Cherry-pick three or four promising locations. Roll them out serially so you can see how to tweak the concept."

"You think they'd let us do it?"

"If the Annex proves out and we have the right business plan they'll at least consider it. Your dad wants a twenty-five percent increase in profitability for Danforth, right? So we propose it to the board in those terms."

Her eyes gleamed. "We just need places with the same demographic."

"There's no reason the concept won't fly in the right markets. Young, rich, hip. It wouldn't be that hard." He took a drink of beer and stared at the ceiling in thought. "Manhattan, of course. That's easy."

"And Miami Beach," she said excitedly. "Rome?"

"Sure. Maybe San Francisco."

"But we'll never give up the flagship store, even when we've achieved world domination in specialty retail."

"We'll never give up the flagship chaise. Some memories should last."

She leaned over to kiss him. "Some memories should."

"Maybe we should make a few more."

And after that, they stopped talking.

14

"TELL ME WHY WE'RE HERE AGAIN?" Rand asked as they walked up to the big warehouse building that was the L.A. Flower Mart. "I thought we were going to see the Lichtenstein retrospective at the art museum."

"We're having Sabrina's shower tomorrow. I told Paige I'd grab some flowers while we were down here."

The doorman took their money and handed Cilla stickers they put on their shirts.

"Why not just call a florist? It'd be easier."

She wrinkled her nose at him. "Because, it's not my party and we're on a budget. You know about budgets, right?" She hooked her hand around his arm.

They stepped through the big open door and Cilla took a deep breath of absolute pleasure. Color, noise and, above all, the almost overpowering scent of hundreds of thousands of flowers. It was a wonderland of blossoms in every hue of the rainbow. Narcissus and freesia, daisies and tulips. Bunches of shocking pink delphiniums sat next to mounds of exuberant orange mums. Spears of stiff white gladiolus stood rigidly upright like soldiers. The bare concrete floor, the functional steel of the building itself were eclipsed by the profusion of colors and sheer lushness of the surroundings.

Everywhere she turned there were stalls crowding the aisles, racks of buckets holding bunches of flowers with little style and scant regard to order. The round magenta blooms of a phalaenopsis orchid bobbed side by side on their flower spike like the smiling faces of 1920s Coca-Cola girls, making her smile in return. For a moment or two, she just wandered, drinking in the sight.

"Paige wants sunflowers, a lot of them, and statice," Cilla said, stopping to sniff some lilacs. "I figured I'd get a few bunches of some other stuff, mums, maybe, or some gerbera daisies."

Rand squinted. "Roses, I know. Sunflowers, thanks to our buddy Vincent. The rest of it, you're on your own."

Cilla laughed and leaned in to kiss him. In the three weeks since the Annex had opened, he'd become more and more a part of her world. Going home to her house alone didn't feel complete anymore. Even an errand as simple as visiting the flower mart was more fun with him along. In the past, serious relationships had always seemed like something to avoid. Casual sex seemed far safer than landing in a situation like that of her parents. Now, though, she couldn't remember the reason to not go for it. Being with Rand felt right, and it was worth finding out just how far right went.

Cilla turned into a stall overflowing with blossoms. She plucked out bunches of yellow sunflowers and stiff stalks of purple statice. "Can I get you to hold some of these?"

Rand gave her an assessing look. "There's a fee."

She raised an eyebrow. "Really?"

"Uh-huh." He tapped his lips.

Fighting a smile, she leaned over to give him a brief peck and handed him the flowers.

They carried the bundles to the back counter, staffed by a whistling man in a green broadcloth apron. He looked just as a flower vendor should, heavyset with sleeves rolled up to his elbows, a bushy dark mustache and twinkling eyes.

"You want some ferns and baby's breath to put in with this? Half price," he offered. He wrapped the flowers up in newspaper and handed them to Rand.

Back out on the floor, she dipped into another stall and emerged with a few stems of blue and gold irises. When they were wrapped, she turned to Rand. "Hold these, will you?"

"Hey, the service ain't free, you know."

Cilla blinked. "I already paid you," she protested.

Rand shook his head, a smile hovering in the corners of his mouth. "Union shop, lady. It's a pay-as-you-go program. You want your flowers held or what?"

"I suppose." Cilla leaned in for another peck, feeling his mouth curve under hers. She held out the flowers, but he didn't take them.

"What, no tip?"

"I paid the fee."

"Yeah, but a guy likes to feel appreciated. Be a shame if I dropped some of these nice flowers."

She rolled her eyes and pressd a hard kiss on him.

"Now that's more like it." Rand grinned broadly.

At the next stall, Cilla turned to him. "Can I pay you in advance?"

Rand shrugged. "Sure, but there's a waiting fee."

"A waiting fee?"

"City sets the schedule, lady. You don't like it, talk to them."

"Well, I never." This time, her lips parted enough to taste him. Not strictly appropriate in a flower mart, probably, but she was sure people would survive.

In high good humor, she wandered in to pick up pink spears of snapdragons, vivid scarlet zinnia, and white phlox, plus another bunch of mums.

Finally, she emerged, with newspaper trumpets of blossoms cradled in her arms.

Rand turned to her. "You going to need assistance getting to your car, lady?"

"I suppose there's a fee for that, too?"

"We offer top service," he reminded her.

"That you do," she murmured, letting the kiss stretch out. When he pulled away, she gave him a look. "I think I have some change coming, don't I?"

"I thought that was the tip," he said quickly.

"It's a little high for a tip, don't you think?"

"Oh, all right," he grumbled and leaned in to linger over her. "There. Oh, and you'll probably want this, too."

He shuffled his bundles and one hand emerged with a small clutch of violets.

"What's that?" she asked, falling out of character.

He smiled. "I thought you deserved some flowers for yourself."

And her heart melted.

"SO, THREE MONTHS until the big day," Kelly told Sabrina. "Getting nervous?" The members of the Supper Club sprawled around Paige's living room, some were curled up on the low, chocolate-brown couches, others sat on the giraffe-patterned rug. The remnants of their brunch sat pillaged on the dining-room table.

Sabrina's eyes danced with amusement under her cap of brown hair. "I figure I already started up a production company with him. Pledging to spend the rest of my life with him is nothing."

"Besides, it gets you wild sex," Cilla pointed out, pushing up the sleeves of her posie-pink sweater. Butterflies made of the same fine-gauge cashmere fluttered up the neckline toward her shoulder. "When did a production company ever do that for you?"

"True."

Paige took a sip of her mimosa. "Okay, everyone, presents," she announced.

"I'll get them." Thea rose to retrieve the small pile of gifts from the dining-room table and brought them over to set on the couch beside Sabrina.

Sabrina picked up a box. "From Delaney to the Bride," she read.

"Keep that one for last," Delaney said hastily.

"I was already planning on it." She picked up another, exquisitely wrapped in nubbly textured paper, with white-and-cream silk ribbons tied around dried flowers. "This has to be from Paige," she said. "I can't bear to destroy the picture yet." She read the tag on another. "Okay, Cilla, how about yours? Any reason I shouldn't open it?"

Cilla shook her head but a little flutter of anticipation went through her. "Have at it."

Sabrina tore off the ribbons and wrappings, revealing the large, flat silver box inside. She pulled off the top and folded back the leaves of tissue paper. And caught her breath.

It was made of gossamer white silk chiffon with a dappling of butterflies in palest green, a peignoir that whispered and settled in the air as she lifted it by the shoulders. Underneath it lay an exquisite merry widow, with delicate lace running along the edges, scalloped where it would brush up against the breasts of the wearer. The others crowded around to see it and to touch.

"Cilla, this is beautiful," Sabrina whispered, holding up the garments one by one. "Did you design this?"

"It's Cilla D., but this is a limited production run. One of a kind, just for you."

"So where do the rest of us get our Cilla D.?" Delaney asked.

"Funny you should ask. The grand opening reception is in a couple of weeks. I'd love to have you guys there. Champagne, music, lingerie," she said, tempting.

Sabrina gave her a hug. "Sounds like my kind of party."

They made her wait to open Delany's gift until she'd gone through the box of bubble bath from Paige, the crotchless undies from Kelly and the book of erotica from Thea and Trish.

"Okay, this is more of a group gift than just from me," Delaney told her, holding out the box, her eyes gleaming.

"I can only imagine what it holds." Sabrina tore cheerfully at the ribbons and paper to reveal a cardboard box packed with lotions and other miscellanea. "Always nice to have one of these," Sabrina said, holding up a sleek vibrator.

"We figured yours might be worn out after all these years," Kelly said.

"What's this?" Sabrina asked, holding up a plastic egg and a remote control emblazoned with a butterfly.

"That's a gift for Stef. Trust me," Cilla said gravely, "you'll love it."

Later, as the party was breaking up, Cilla dialed Rand on her cell phone. "Hey, gorgeous, what are you up to?"

"Nothing nearly as exciting as I would be if you were here. Thinking about going for a bike ride, maybe. How about you?"

She could hear the outdoor sounds coming through the phone and could picture him on his balcony. "We're just about finished here."

"Have fun?"

"Oh, it was great. Sabrina says Stef's going to love the egg."

He laughed. "I know I did. So what are you doing after?"

"I guess that depends on you. I have to do some odds and ends and then I was just going to hang. I don't suppose you'd like some company, would you?"

"That'd be much more exciting than a bike ride," he said immediately.

"I think so, too." She wondered when she'd stop getting butterflies at the thought of seeing him. "Look, I've got to help Paige clean up a little and stop by my apartment to get some clothes. It's what, two? Give me a couple hours."

"Around four?"

Cilla smiled. "I'll be there with bells on."

"And nothing else, I hope."

"Guess you'll just have to wait and find out."

IT WASN'T UNTIL MUCH LATER, when she was headed to Rand's, that she realized the time. She couldn't pinpoint, exactly, where the hours had gone, but what with one thing and another, four had turned to six and later, and the afternoon was fading to dusk. Of course, it wasn't as though they'd had actual plans, she reminded herself. He'd never minded before when she'd shown up late. He knew she wasn't good at estimating time. It was just a couple of hours, it didn't really matter.

But when he opened the door, it was clear it did.

"Sorry I'm late." Diving in was probably best.

He stood back to let her in. "Did something come up?"

"Not really." She set down her bags. "I wound up doing a couple of errands on my way home after the shower, and took care of some stuff at the house, and my mom called, so I talked with her for a bit. You know, usual Sunday-afternoon stuff." Suddenly uncomfortable, Cilla trailed off. "What have you been up to?"

Rand shrugged. "Hanging, mostly, waiting for you to show up."

It made her feel guilty, and crowded. "But we didn't have plans."

"No," he said evenly. "On the other hand, I couldn't very well leave when you were supposed to be here and I didn't know when you were going to show up."

"You're ticked off."

"I'm…frustrated. I could have gone grocery shopping, or for a bike ride, even."

"I thought you'd just be watching the game," she said, bewildered. "I didn't think it mattered that I took a little extra time."

"But it did, and now the day's blown and the weekend's over."

Her bags still sat in the entryway. She suddenly didn't feel much like moving them. How had she wound up accountable for every minute of her time? As much as she loved being with Rand, it was okay to have a few minutes to herself, wasn't it? It wasn't that she hadn't shown up, she'd just lost track of time. Weekends were supposed to be about puttering.

And yet, somehow it was as if she'd done something wrong.

"I don't know how to feel about this," she began, picking her way carefully. "It's like I've done something bad, and yet I don't really think I did. All I did was spend a little time doing some odds and ends, on my time, on a weekend. It's not like we had tickets or reservations or plans to meet someone." She twisted at the thick chain bracelet that encircled her wrist. "I feel like somehow I'm on a schedule or something. I don't want to feel trapped, but I…" To her horror, she felt tears welling up and she walked toward the slider that led to his balcony.

Outside, the air was warm and dry, the sky still clear this early in the summer. She leaned on the railing.

Rand came up behind her. "Cilla." His voice was soft as he leaned on the railing next to her. "I'm not trying to tell you how to spend your time or what you're supposed to do. We don't have to spend every moment together. Of course you need time to yourself to get things done. I do, too." He took her hand and drew her down to one of the chairs. "All you had to do was call and tell me you were running late and you'd be over later, or not at all, even. That simple." His eyes were dark and serious. "I'm not trying to trap you. But as long as we're involved, what you do has an effect on me. I'm just asking you to think about that."

It was like looking at a 3-D picture when a swirl of color suddenly turned into leaping dolphins or something. Except that in this case it wasn't leaping dolphins but the realization that he was right. Guilt pricked at her.

"I'm sorry. I...I never thought about it like that," she blurted. She watched a car thread its way up a road in the Hollywood Hills, searching for its way. Like her. Biting her lip, she looked at Rand. "I've never been in this kind of relationship before. It's mostly been casual dating. You know, go out to a club, go to a concert. I'm not used to spending all my time with someone." She hesitated. "I'm not used to having to account for my time."

"I'm not trying—"

She held up a hand. "Let me finish, okay. This, what's between us, is really important to me, and I want to be with you. It's only when I have a few minutes to myself that I start remembering all the things that need to be done." She swallowed. It was important that he understood. It was important to get it right. "That's why I was late today. I never thought about it as tying up your time, and I'm sorry. This is new territory for me."

Rand stirred. "Maybe it's new territory for both of us." He leaned forward and caught her hands in his. "The last thing I want is for you to feel trapped. Look, I'm nuts about you and I want to spend time with you, but not if you're feeling hemmed in. Take the time to do what you need to."

"I'll be better about this in the future, I promise." She slanted him a look. "So, nuts, huh? Could you be a little more specific?"

He drew her to her feet. "I could demonstrate, if you want."

"I certainly hope so."

15

RAND LOOKED at his watch. Grand opening day. Somehow, when he hadn't been paying attention, over a month had whisked by since they'd opened the doors at the Annex. Maybe he hadn't been paying attention to the calendar because he'd been paying attention to Cilla, instead.

The telephone on Rand's desk burbled. Absently, he reached out and picked it up. "Rand Mitchell," he said, without pausing in his work.

"Hello, Rand, this is Elliot Patterson, with Stratosphere Executive Recruiters. How are you doing?"

"Fine." He waited.

"You don't remember me, do you?"

Rand didn't, and yet the name rang a faint bell. And then his mental search engine brought it up. Elliot Patterson, a headhunter who'd tried to recruit him when he was at his dot-com job. A different employer, but then a lot of them were at different employers these days. "It's been a while, Elliot. How have you been?"

"Scrapping a little but things have been getting better."

"Glad to hear it." But he knew this wasn't a social call, and Elliot proved him right.

"I'm calling because we've got an opportunity that might be a very good fit for you. Do you have a few minutes to talk?"

Rand's first impulse was to say no and hang up. The grand opening's reception for the Annex started in less than three hours and he had a meeting, a telecon and a couple of e-mails to deal with before he'd be free to leave. He didn't have time for recruiters. Still, a smart man always listened. You never knew when the hot opportunity was going to fall in your lap, and you never knew when a connection you made today might become important. He checked his watch. "I've got five minutes before I have to be in a meeting. What's on your mind?"

"I was surprised to hear that you'd gone into retail. You seem like such a good fit for high tech. How's it working out for you in the bricks-and-mortar world?"

"The bricks-and-mortar world is producing a paycheck," he responded. "I like it just fine."

"You don't miss life on the cutting edge?"

It made Rand impatient. "Five minutes, Elliot. Who is it and what is it?"

Elliot laughed. "Same old Mitchell. Listen, I've got a venture capital fund up in Silicon Valley. They're looking to get their money working and they're looking for someone to manage it. You know, help them latch onto the next big thing."

"Tell them to get in line."

"That's just the thing, they don't want to get in line. They want to be there first and they're looking for someone to spearhead the project."

It raised a flicker of interest, but only a flicker. "Private or institutional?"

"Private. A dozen investors who want to get their money working."

"VC isn't the slam dunk it was in the nineties," Rand warned him. "What's to stop them from losing their enthusiasm?"

Patterson chuckled. "A very generous five-year contract with the managing partner, for one. Interested in hearing more?"

Rand glanced at his watch. "I might be, but not right now."

"When? These guys know your record and they're very eager to meet you."

"Let me think about it over the weekend and get back to you Monday. Give me your number and I'll call you when I've got some time to talk."

He hung up the phone, already reaching out for the file he needed for his meeting. The five minutes had stretched to ten, making him late. Great, he thought, walking out of his office as he flipped open the folder to check his spot on the agenda.

And barreled right into a young woman from the mail room carrying one of those complicated frappuccino-whipped-cream-whatevers from the coffee bar on the ground floor.

A complicated whatever that wound up all over him.

"Ohmigod, I'm so sorry," she blurted, aghast, staring at the brown splotch that ran from his chest to crotch, and dripped slowly into a puddle on the ground.

Good thing it was iced, Rand thought. "Don't worry about it, I should have been watching where I was going."

"I can get some napkins from the break room," she offered anxiously.

"It's okay, really." The last thing he needed was some intern mopping his crotch. Anyway, it was going to take a whole lot more than a napkin or two to fix his clothes.

So much for getting to the grand opening early.

Stifling his frustration, Rand ducked into the men's room to dry off the worst of it. Fortunately, little of the coffee had made it onto the documents inside. Uncomfortable as it might be, he really ought to do the meeting.

Right, new plan. Skip the telecons, skip the e-mail, see if he could get pushed forward in the agenda and head home to change before the reception.

"May you live in interesting times" was a Chinese curse, he thought with a sigh, and headed more moderately down the hall to the conference room.

THERE WAS A REASON she never had parties on weeknights, Cilla thought as she glanced at her computer clock for the hundredth time. The last thing she wanted was to be stuck at work when she knew she had high-stakes entertaining to do. It would be so much easier to have done it on a Saturday night. Unfortunately, Saturday night wouldn't allow the journalists to get the events into their fashion sections, whereas the weeknight would.

She wanted to be at the Annex, hovering over the decorations, the food, the music. It didn't matter that they'd secured one of the top party planners in L.A. to arrange the whole event. Cilla needed to be on-site to do her ritual dithering, to calm her nerves, if nothing else.

The Annex wasn't her only job, though. Danforth and Forth's needed stock. Orders had to go out on time or else the shipments wouldn't arrive with the season. And when it came to couture, timing was everything.

With an eye on the clock, she reviewed her order files. Making herself go slowly was the hardest part, but eventually it was done and she e-mailed the file off to her assistant. A fraction before five, Cilla thought jubilantly. She had her outfit with her so that she could change, spruce up and still get over to the Annex in plenty of time.

There was too much riding on the success of this night.

Poor Rand, she thought as she locked herself into a stall in the bathroom, having to run all the way home to change.

Cilla wriggled into her complicated Helmut Lang top, focusing on getting the wide band of stretchy white jersey wrapped around her shoulder blades just right so that she could bring it forward to cover her breasts—that part was important—before threading it through the black hoop that hung from her neck and pulling it down taut to cover her belly. She slid the fabric into the skin-tight black mini that went with the outfit, which would leave her—she hoped—decently covered. She should have been smart enough to bring some of J. Lo's double sticky tape to hold it in place. Instead, she tucked the fabric more securely into her skirt and reminded herself not to make any sudden moves.

Going from day to night with cosmetics was a bit more time-consuming when the party guests included the fashion press and photographers. Fortunately, she had a skilled hand with makeup. A little more dramatic on the eyes, a little more vivid on the lips, and all she needed was a spritz of perfume to be ready to go.

Not bad, Cilla thought, surveying herself in the mirror as she hooked swingy silver loops through her ears. Not bad at all.

She was back in her office fishing out her purse when her administrative assistant poked her head through the door.

She hesitated. "I know you're trying to get going, but the big chief wants you to stop in his office."

Cilla glanced at the clock. Five-fifteen. She looked back at Renee, who didn't move.

"Today, he said." Her eyes were sympathetic, but clearly she wasn't going to let Cilla off the hook and risk getting in hot water herself.

With a sigh, Cilla picked up her bag and headed down the hall. Was it her imagination, or did the carpet really get plusher as she walked into the executive quarter? Certainly the artwork was higher quality. As to the offices…

She knocked on the open oak door of her father's half-acre office. "You wanted to see me?"

He blinked at her outfit. "Isn't that a little much for the office?"

"You're right, it is." Cilla laughed. "Relax, I just changed into it. It's for the Annex. The grand opening reception is tonight. Are you going to make it?"

He made an impatient noise. "Probably not. The board meeting is tomorrow, so I've got dinner with Burt and the rest."

Was it time for that already? It made Cilla's head spin a little to think of it. "Bring the board with you.

You can see what we've done with the place. We should have quite a crowd."

"Happy to hear it."

"Happy to hear it, but, you mean," she said slowly, knowing what was going to come next. He wasn't even going to give her the six months. He was going to pull the plug before they had a chance to make it go, just as she'd put everything she had behind making the store work. He was going to kill it before they'd even fully seen what it could do.

She waited, fighting the urge to fidget.

Her father gave her a level look. "You know I wasn't in agreement with keeping that store open."

"I know." She could stay just as poker-faced as he could.

"And I certainly wasn't in favor of turning it over to you to revamp. I didn't think you'd have the skill or the discipline to pull it off, even with help."

Hadn't she done enough to please him? Cilla wondered. Would she ever? "And what do you think now?"

"I think you've done quite well with it."

A beat went by. "You what?" she repeated blankly.

"It just goes to show that even I can be wrong." A flicker of humor entered his eyes.

She had to be hearing things. Had he just given her an attaboy? "Could you repeat that, please?"

"What, that I can be wrong?"

"No, the part where you tell me I've done a good job." She smiled faintly. "I could get used to this."

"I knew you had a certain skill with buying, but that's more about anticipating trends. It's not project management."

"I did project management in school." She was careful to keep her voice calm.

"School and the real world are two different things."

"I know. That's why I wanted the chance to see what I could do." *And to show you,* she added silently.

"Well, we're all seeing it. Your revenue numbers are definitely going in the right direction. You've beat your first month projections, but then I'm sure you know that."

Cilla flushed with pleasure. "We could never have done it if we hadn't gotten the go-ahead from you, not to mention the money."

"Stewart Law got the go-ahead and money, too, and look what he did with it," he reminded her. "Your strategy looks promising right out of the gate."

"We need to make sure it holds," she said uneasily. They should be cautious about celebrating too much before they had more time in to be sure it was real. An unholy flutter in her gut told her it was, though.

"It'll hold." He steepled his fingers. "I thought it was an impossible timeline. And halfway into it, you've proved me wrong."

"We've proved you wrong," she corrected. "Rand has had a hand in this all the way. He should get credit, too."

"No doubt. The question now is what comes next."

Of course. It always was with her father. *Plan to beat what your competition's grandson is going to do,* he was fond of saying. An admirable focus, but it was also possible to get too far ahead. "The store's only been open for a month, Dad. We need to be sure it's got staying power before we think about anything else."

"You need to be focusing on making it work and on what comes next. You have to have thought about it. You're too much my daughter not to."

It gave her a little jolt of pleasure. "We've talked about it some."

"What have you got up your sleeve?"

"Spinouts. If it works, the next thing to do is pick a couple of likely locations and expand."

"In L.A., you mean?"

She shook her head. "Miami Beach, say, and Manhattan for starters. Then we move out to international locations—Milan, Paris, Berlin. Places with the right demographic. Break out slow, build buzz, and then broaden."

For a moment, he just stared at her.

Cilla shifted in her chair. "What?"

"I underestimated you," he said slowly. "Looks like I have been for a long time."

She flushed with pride.

"Well, no more," he said briskly. "Starting now. The board meeting is tomorrow. I have your project status report, but I want something outlining your thoughts going forward."

"What, for the L.A. store?"

He smiled briefly. "No. For your chain."

She checked her watch. "I have to get to the opening."

"It's not even five-thirty." He dismissed her concern. "Your opening doesn't start until what, six? Seven?"

"Seven," she admitted.

"And, anyway, you've got people there, don't you? You need to remember to delegate."

"I have," she assured him.

"Then you've got time. All I need is for you to bang out a one pager for tonight so that I can get them thinking about it. You can still be on your way by six."

The words were already forming in her head as she hurried back to her office.

16

IT WAS SORT OF LIKE CHEMISTRY, Cilla thought. You put the right combination of things together—in this case, music, liquor, stylish people—and you got something that bubbled and fizzed. By any standards, the party was a success. On a temporary waist-high catwalk threaded down the middle of the store, models strutted in Cilla D. and designs by L.A.'s up-and-comers. At the back, tables covered in snow-white linen and crowned by ice sculptures held trays of oysters, tuna ceviche and crudités. Waiters dressed in black circulated with trays of crab puffs and Thai egg rolls. A statuesque woman tended bar. The sound of chatter and laughter rose and fashionistas from Hollywood and the music industry milled around the room.

Cilla had been juggling interviews for much of the night. At the Video Style Awards, she'd teased them with the prospect. Now, she had them all to herself in one room for the real thing.

Across the way, Rand spoke with a reporter for *L.A. Weekly,* who definitely looked a bit starry-eyed as she wrote down his answers to her questions. Not that Cilla could blame her. He wore a Versace jacket over a band-collar black shirt and jeans, a more casual, hipper look than his usual sleekly stylish Armani. He'd left his five o'clock shadow in place when he'd gone home to change. The dark of his jaw turned the gray of his eyes to silver.

Cilla walked toward the front of the store, pausing to exchange air kisses with a fashion-mad indie actress she'd gotten to know at runway shows. "That should show up in a couple of national publications," Cilla said in satisfaction to Paige as she came to a stop beside her. "Chloë always shows up in the party pages."

"Free press is free press," said Paige, self-possessed, as usual, in a narrow honey-colored sheath. "Now, if Trish and Ty were here, you'd be set."

"Darn these actors and screenwriters, always worried about making movies." Cilla watched an editor from *Vogue* sink down on one of the chaises. "Of course, the design and the artwork make the whole place."

"I noticed you had a couple of the artists here tonight."

"Why not treat it like an opening? The more buzz the better, as far as I'm concerned. It was a great idea," Cilla said frankly.

A corner of Paige's mouth quirked. "You'll be getting the bill." She surveyed the room. "So, what does the press think about the stock in the boudoir?"

Cilla nibbled her lip. "I put it out of sight," she confessed. "I'd rather have it get out by word of mouth."

"Probably safer."

"What's safer?" Delaney inquired. She wore a stretchy-knit dress in a beach umbrella stripe. Her white blond hair swung loose down past her shoulder blades. Sabrina and Thea trailed after her.

"Hiding the toys."

Thea nodded. "What daddy and the board don't know won't hurt them."

A waiter stopped by with a tray of hot hors d'oeuvres and Sabrina picked up a crab puff. "It's about time we got you away from the reporters so that we can grill you. So what's the deal with that man of yours?"

"He's pretty hot, even by your standards," Delaney added, and popped a bit of smoked salmon topped with caviar into her mouth.

Sabrina eyed Cilla speculatively. "This looks a lot more serious than you made it sound."

It made her uneasy to think about it. When she was with Rand, it seemed natural for them to be getting more and more involved. She couldn't imagine doing anything else. When she was away from him, it was a little more alarming, in terms of how deep their connection went. She'd grown up mistrusting relationships because of her parents. She'd kept all of hers light, intentionally. When she'd leaped into the casual affair with Rand, she'd never expected it to be more than good times, great sex. Or if she'd had an inkling of anything more, she'd steadfastly ignored it.

Now, as the weeks had turned into a month, then two, that was becoming a more and more difficult exercise.

She looked at Sabrina, at the rest of the gang. She knew they would understand anything she told them, but she wasn't sure she understood herself right then.

"Right now, he's great. I can't think about where it goes from here." It was true, so much as she said.

"You let that one get away, you've got a hole in

your head," Delaney said. "He scores very high on the Supper Club-o-Meter."

"We did take a vote," Sabrina told her. "He gets the official seal of approval."

"He'll be relieved to hear it," Cilla said.

"He'll be relieved to hear what?" Rand asked from behind her.

Cilla jumped and shot a glare at Sabrina opposite her, who just gave her a saintly smile. "That you've gotten the vote of confidence from the gang, here."

Some men would have been embarrassed. Rand just seemed amused. "Good thing. I can sleep tonight," he said easily. "The reporter from the *Times* is waiting to interview us, so I need to borrow Cilla for a minute."

"Somehow I don't think there's going to be too much sleeping going on," Sabrina murmured to Paige as the pair of them walked away.

THE WOMAN FROM THE FASHION PAGE of the *Times* was rail thin and dressed in a luscious silver-and-black knit from St. Johns. "I have to hand it to you, Danforth certainly knows how to do it up right," she said, drink in one silver-tipped hand, recorder in another. "It's certainly not customary for even upscale boutiques."

It was precisely the effect Cilla had hoped for. "We wanted to send the message that something different is going on here."

"That much is certainly true. The art is an interesting move. Are you anticipating that that will be an important part of the store?"

"It's a bit like having musicians play at a bookstore," Rand told her. "We know the art will more than likely appeal to the design aesthetic of our customers. Will we sell some? Probably, but it won't be the mainstay of our business. That's fashion."

The reporter nodded. "Danforth Annex was a disappointing performer, by all accounts. What makes you think the reinvention will work this time?"

"It'll succeed because of a new approach in everything from the stock to the look," Cilla explained. "We're not taking Danforth on a road show, we're building a different store for a whole separate clientele. It's our chance to carry some edgier stock, highlight some of the up-and-coming designers who are taking chances."

"Designers like Cilla D., for example?" the woman asked, fingering the silk of one of Cilla's more outrageous concoctions. "Now that you've released the line, what other retailers are going to carry it?"

"Nobody. The Annex is going to be the exclusive source."

"A single store in a single city?" The reporter's eyebrows rose. "You can't expect to get far with such a limited distribution."

"As the Annex grows, Cilla D. will grow."

"You're expecting to expand the Annex?" The reporter's gaze sharpened.

"There's a demand for a store like this in multiple markets," Cilla told her. "As to whether we're going to expand, well, that'll have to wait until it makes sense. Excuse me." She turned to greet box-office queen Megan Barnes, catching both her hands and kissing her on the cheek, then posing for a photo.

"Sorry about that. Are there any other questions I can answer?"

The *Times* reporter's eyes were bright. "No, this will do nicely."

"You should be careful talking too much about the spin-out idea," Rand murmured to Cilla. "People are likely to—"

A tall, white-haired man with a basso voice interrupted them. "Excuse me, Rand? Tom Montgomery from the *Journal*. I interviewed you back when you were with B2B.com."

"Right." Rand shook hands with him. "Glad you could make it. Meet Cilla Danforth, who's my in-house partner on the project."

He made the usual nice noises of greeting, but Cilla could see his focus was on Rand. She gave them both a brilliant smile. "I'm sure you two want to catch up. I'll leave you to it." She turned away, then her mouth curved in surprised pleasure. "Uncle Burt," she cried out, crossing to him, eyes bright.

He wrapped her in a bear hug. "Got no patience for those damned air kisses people do at these things."

Cilla stepped back from him, smiling. "What are you doing here? Did my father come?" she asked before she could help herself. The look of annoyed regret on his face told her the answer, though.

Burt shook his head. "I left those sad sacks at the board dinner."

She should have known better than to expect her father to show, Cilla thought. He had better things to do. He always had better things to do. "Won't they excommunicate you for leaving early?" she asked, struggling to hide her disappointment.

"That? Hell, that wasn't a board meeting. It was

just an excuse to tell tall tales and guzzle expensive wine on an expense account. I wasn't about to sit around there with them when the biggest party event of the year was going on. Besides," he leaned in to confide, "my personal trainer would just kill me if I had had dessert. My carb count would go through the roof."

Cilla stared. "Uncle Burt, you, too? Say it's not so. Tell me you haven't gone Atkins and gotten a personal trainer," she pleaded.

He winked. "I haven't. I just heard it three times walking across the room to get to you, so I figured I'd try it out. Show you how hip I am."

Cilla threw back her head and laughed, as he'd probably intended. He'd always been able to make her feel good, always. "I've never doubted your hipness, Uncle Burt."

"I'm so proud of you tonight, Cilla. Your father is, too, even if he's not here. You should have heard him bragging on you tonight to the rest of the guys. We all know the numbers." He gave her a fond look. "You've just done a champion job with this project, a champion job."

"I didn't do it alone," she reminded him, basking in his praise.

"I know, I know, you had your partner, but it's a lot of your hard work and inspiration, too. You do us proud," he told her, "you do us proud."

It made her want to tear up, it felt so good, and she leaned in to hug him again. He'd always known just what to say to her to make things right.

Burt patted her cheek and tucked her hand through his arm. "Now, give me the grand tour," he said comfortably.

So she started at the front of the store and worked her way to the back, showing him the various innovations, pointing out changes planned for the future. He wasn't just there to give unqualified acceptance, she understood; his questions were penetrating, his capacity for detail endless. He scanned the art with the eye of a connoisseur and gave it a ringing endorsement. He surveyed the clothing with more of a focus on the display fixtures. He looked hastily away from the models wearing Cilla D., and Cilla grinned.

"Uncle Burt, are you blushing?"

"They're young enough to be my granddaughters," he muttered. "I'm not going to stare at my granddaughters naked."

"I guess that means you're not going to get them Annex gift certificates for their birthdays, hmm?"

"Oh, I'll do that," he assured her, busying himself with a tray of canapés passing by. "I just don't want to know how they spend it."

"Careful with those appetizers. Remember your personal trainer."

Burt winked. "What she doesn't know won't hurt her."

"She?" Cilla raised an eyebrow.

"Hey, if she's imaginary, my trainer can be anything I want."

Cilla laughed, delighted, then noticed a Dolce & Gabbana–clad woman hovering nearby. Interviews, she thought with resignation, glancing at her watch.

"Got to get back to it?" Burt asked, not missing their shadow.

Cilla nodded. "The editor from *Women's Wear*

Daily," she murmured, leaning in to kiss his cheek. "Gotta make nice."

"No one better than you to do it."

She hugged him. "It was such fun to have you show up here tonight, Uncle Burt. You're wonderful."

And she turned to the editor. It didn't matter that the questions were the same as the past four interviews she'd done.

Circulating was the key, Cilla thought as she chatted with the woman. Same questions, same responses. She could see how celebrities got tired of it after a while.

Then Rand walked by with the *Journal* reporter. For a moment he caught Cilla's eye and gave her one of those smiles meant for her alone. Something in her jolted and for a moment it was as though the whole scene paused. The lips of the *Women's Wear Daily* editor moved but nothing she said registered. Cilla gave her a meaningless smile, not knowing how to tell her that her life had completely changed in the blink of an eye, the flash of a smile. "I'm sorry, could you please repeat that question?" she said instead. After all, how did you tell someone that a look across the room had changed everything?

How did you tell them that you'd realized you were in love?

THE LONG NIGHT was over.

They walked into Rand's foyer. It was as though she were walking on foam rubber in stilettos, this feeling that nothing underfoot was solid or steady. At the same time, she felt buoyed up. Silly, she chastised herself. It certainly wasn't what they'd agreed on when they'd launched into this affair. It made her more than a little nervous. What if he didn't love her back? What did people in love do? How did it change things? She'd seen Sabrina and Kelly and Trish go through it, but their affairs were new. She'd seen what could happen.

And yet she'd seen it could work, she'd noticed Rand's parents, the moments in which the depth of their feeling for one another was nearly palpable.

"You okay?" Rand asked. "You've been pretty quiet."

"I'm just exhausted," she said truthfully, walking over to the slider to stare out at the lights.

He walked over to put his arms around her from behind. "You should be proud of yourself." He kissed her hair. "Tonight went incredibly well."

"It did. We both should be proud of ourselves." She turned in his arms to face him. "It's going to be a success, Rand."

"It already is."

He kissed her and the kiss flowed through her body, liquefying her muscles. Was it just different because of the awareness that now flowered in her? Was it different because they had built something together?

She wasn't ready to trust the words or the feeling, but she could show him. She couldn't pledge her heart but she could touch him. And in a room lit only by moonlight and the faint light in the foyer, they came together in tenderness, the slow grace of it like emotion brought to life. The slide of hand over skin, the touch of lips to body, the act was a sacrament, the slow shudders of orgasm irrelevant. And when he slipped inside her, they were one.

17

CILLA SAT IN HER OFFICE as the morning wore away, trying to knock items off her to-do list even as she found herself interrupted by congratulatory phone calls about the Annex and updates from the store manager. Unfortunately, focusing on any of it was nearly impossible. She hadn't slept much of the night, probing at her newly realized feelings like a loose tooth. She wasn't sure what to do about them. She wasn't sure how she felt about, well, how she felt. As the morning wore away, though, she became increasingly certain of one thing: she had to talk with Rand.

It would be okay, she told herself. Two things she knew she could expect from him were tolerance and patience. He would understand if she told him about her feelings, even if she didn't completely understand them herself. She had to tell him.

If she could just find the nerve.

Cilla groped for her coffee cup, hoping more caffeine might help her fight off the leaden fatigue. Her phone rang. She wondered briefly how the board meeting was going, and she groaned. She'd forgotten to tell Rand about the memo. He ought to at least know they were going to be on the hot seat, given that they were on the agenda to report on the Annex just before lunch. She reached out for the telephone receiver just as a cadaverously thin woman barged into her office.

It was the head of the couture department at Danforth, an excitable ex-model with snow-white hair swept back from her face. "There's a problem with the Yamamoto trunk show."

"We'll take care of it, Simone," Cilla soothed. "If you'll just give me a minute."

"Give you a minute?" Her voice rose. "I'm going to have a department full of people in exactly," she checked her watch, "six hours, and the merchandise is still held up in customs."

"I just have one phone call to make and I'll get in touch."

"No." Simone stood before the desk ready to go into a classic meltdown, and Cilla gave up all hope of being able to do a single thing before Simone's crisis was dealt with. By the time she'd sorted everything out, sending a flurry of faxes and making crack-of-dawn phone calls to Tokyo, getting the local customs officials involved, she was already late for her slot at the board meeting and her grace period with Rand had gone. It would be all right, she reassured herself. He'd understand.

"Okay, Simone, everything's taken care of with customs. I've got to go speak with the board."

Simone's nostrils flared. So long as she had to rely on others to solve her problems, she was unlikely to ever deal with the board, Cilla thought, stifling a sigh as she walked down to the conference room.

Rand was already there, waiting for her.

The room was paneled in walnut and lit from above. The enormous ebony-colored slab of the conference table gleamed with polish. Abstract art—original— adorned the back wall. The board sat around the table in deep leather chairs, looking as if they ought to be smoking cigars and drinking port. Sitting among them, Rand looked right at home.

Cilla took the empty seat next to him.

"Here they are, the whiz kids," Burt Ruxton said with a smile. "You two have done quite a job with your project."

"I see we made the nationals." Bernard Fox held up the newspapers, each folded to the story. "I have to say, when I first heard about the party idea I thought it was a waste of dollars, but I see the value now. Excellent exposure for the project. For Danforth and Forth's, also, for that matter."

"The exposure's good," her father agreed. "The revenue reports are better."

"The exposure's going to make the revenue reports shoot through the roof," Cilla assured him. "We've already seen a jump in sales this morning, according to the store manager. Several of the pieces of artwork went last night, and we've had inquiries about others."

"We aren't trying to run a gallery," her father rumbled.

"Any revenue we get from the art is just gravy," Rand pointed out. "The value is in the cachet it gives the Annex and the quality of customer it attracts."

"And it's working," Cilla said firmly. "If you take a look at the numbers for the first six weeks of operation, you can see we're ahead of budget despite outlays for redecorating and restocking."

Paper flapped as the board examined the documents. Cilla waited. Fox glanced up at her. "Well executed. The key, though, is going to be holding to the curve."

"Considering that the current set of numbers has only been fueled by word of mouth, I'm confident of that." It was working, she thought jubilantly. The project was a success.

"The other thing you'll find in this section is the strategic plan going forward," Danforth said. "Cilla, here, has an idea about spinning the store out into a chain, assuming its current success continues."

Rand whipped his head around to stare at Cilla, and she felt a sudden twist of anxiety.

The board members studied the memo for a few minutes. Fox nodded. "I like your direction. It's good to see you thinking this far ahead, Cilla."

"My daughter knows my feeling about advance planning," Danforth said.

"Some good work, here," Ruxton approved. "You've put together the outline of a very nice plan."

"We did," she corrected tightly, "Rand and I."

"If the project stays ahead of target by the end of the probationary period, I think we need to give serious thought to a timeline for moving forward on this," her father said. "Cilla, I want you to put together a full business plan on this. Use Rand to help you as necessary."

Panic shot through her veins. They kept talking about it coming from her alone, but that couldn't be right, could it? She racked her brains to remember the lines she'd dashed out the night before. The memo had been from her standard template, but she was sure she'd indicated both of them as the source. She had to have said that it was work they'd done together.

Work they'd done as a team.

Rand's face was expressionless. "May I see that memo, please?" he asked Ruxton pleasantly.

Burt handed it over.

Cilla watched Rand's face, holding her breath. As he scanned the sheet, his jaw tightened.

And she knew.

"I'd like a quick rundown of any changes you're looking to make to the store at this point, based on results to date," her father commented.

Cilla turned to Rand, but he just inclined his head. "Please, take over by all means. It's your show."

"RAND, IT WAS A MISTAKE." Cilla hurried down the hall after him, almost tripping as her heel caught in the plush carpet. "They got it wrong."

"Someone did."

When they'd finished talking to the board—when she'd finished, really, since Rand had remained silent—he'd risen and left as though he were alone. She refused to run after him. She couldn't let him go on thinking that he'd let her down, though. Surely once she explained he'd understand.

Surely.

Rand didn't turn into his office as she'd expected, but kept walking down the hallway to the elevator, fury vibrating through his body. He hit the call button with the heel of his hand.

"Rand, talk to me," she hissed, glancing around to see if anyone was nearby. Far down the hallway, her father and the rest of the board emerged from the conference room. The elevator dinged and the doors swept back. "Where are you going?" she asked

He didn't answer, just walked into the car. Cilla stepped in behind him, even as the doors closed. "Look, it was an accident," she said, relieved to have a few moments of privacy. "I didn't mean it to come off that way."

"I'm sure."

"He hit me up for the memo last night when I was leaving for the reception," she blurted. "I just whipped it out without thinking. I wasn't trying to take credit for your work. I'm sorry."

"Of course."

"I forgot about it because of the reception and because of some things I was busy thinking about. Some things I'd like to talk with you about later."

He didn't even respond to that, just stood waiting until the elevator doors opened, the tension building in his shoulders. "Will you stop a minute and listen to me?" Cilla demanded, chasing after him as he walked through the lobby and outside with his ground-eating strides.

"For what?" he spat out. "To hear you apologize another time before you turn around and do it all over again?"

"I said I was sorry," she reminded him, with the beginnings of irritation.

"You're always sorry, Cilla, and it's always an accident. You didn't think about it, you didn't mean it, it didn't occur to you. Well somehow, somewhere along the line it should goddamn well start to." He swung around to face her and his eyes were bright with anger. And betrayal, she saw.

"It was a memo, Rand. I can't believe you're getting this bent out of shape over a piece of paper. It was a misunderstanding."

"It's not the fucking memo, Cilla," he said furiously. "Don't you get it? It goes a lot deeper than that. It's about you flying solo, you thinking solo. It's supposed to be us, remember? How many times have we had this conversation?"

Her cheeks and lips felt numb with the force of his anger. Even when she'd known he was irritated before, he'd always held on to control. He'd always been reasonable. Now, his fury was loose, palpable, whipping around her like a windstorm.

"We keep talking, you keep being sorry, and nothing changes. And I'm an idiot because I tell myself that you'll start to get it, that you'll remember that I'm a part of this, too. I keep telling myself that you'll start thinking of us as a team, but it's starting to look like that's never going to happen."

"Of course it's going to happen. I do think of us as a team."

"Really?" Abruptly, his anger cooled to ice. "You have a funny way of showing it."

"Rand, don't be like this," she said desperately, even as his words sliced into her. "I was in a hurry, that's all. We can straighten this out. I wasn't trying to ambush you."

He gave a humorless laugh. "The sick thing is that I believe you. I don't think you were trying to screw me over, I think it just didn't occur to you. And you know what? That makes it worse."

"It was a mistake."

"And it's always a mistake with you, isn't it," he said tiredly.

She licked her lips. "I'm not used to thinking in pairs."

"You've used that one up already, Cilla."

And suddenly her own anger rose at his tone. "What, there's a project timeline on me, now? Do I have milestones to meet? And what happens then, do I get a bonus? This can't all happen on your schedule, Rand."

"Look—" he rounded on her "—the reality is that you don't think beyond yourself. You don't understand what being part of a couple is all about. We keep coming back to the same thing, time after time. You say you're going to change, but there's always something that comes up. Well, I'm tired of things coming up."

"You're not the only judge of what a relationship is about," she burst out, trembling. "You're not the project leader here. This is supposed to be about us, right?"

He stared at her. "It was supposed to be." And he turned on his heel and walked away.

AND HE WALKED, for the better part of an hour he walked. He itched to go run, to lift weights, to do something to burn off the anger that jittered through him. But all he could do was walk. And when he'd used up as much time as he could justify, given the things on his desk clamoring for attention, he made himself return to the Danforth building.

He did his best to look the other way as he passed Cilla's office. Now that the first flare of emotion was gone, he ached for her. It would be so easy to turn through that door, to talk about it, to get past it.

To hold her again.

He could do that. He could let it go, but then again, he'd let it go time after time and the only change was no change at all. Maybe he needed to accept the fact that no matter how much he might love her, deep down, they didn't fit.

Just as Danforth didn't fit. It never had. And he wasn't at all sure he could come to work every day and see Cilla, or even hear of her through the company grapevine, and not go crazy. It was time for a change, pure and simple. It was time for change in a lot of ways.

He picked up the phone and dialed the headhunter.

18

CILLA SAT AT THE SUN-WASHED TABLE before her French doors, trying to focus on the drawings. She needed to expand the Cilla D. line in order to support the runway show during Fall Fashion Week in New York. Designing took energy. It took concentration. And if she focused on it hard enough, maybe she could manage to stop thinking about Rand for just one minute.

She closed her eyes to imagine the lines of the new negligee she was sketching. Instead, she saw the disgusted look in Rand's eyes as he'd turned away from her. She blinked the tears furiously away. She should be angry, not hurt. He'd totally misunderstood the situation, and hadn't even tried to give her the benefit of the doubt. That was what she should be thinking about, not the cutting tone in his voice, not the set of his shoulders as he'd walked away.

He'd gotten frustrated before, but they'd gotten past it. She concentrated on that fact, held on to it like a talisman even as her hand shook and she dropped her pencil. Sooner or later, he'd come to her and they'd talk. Of course he'd come to her. He'd apologize, he'd accept her apology, and they'd go forward.

But then, that had been what she'd told herself the

afternoon of the board meeting, and that night she'd stayed by the phone and waited. But Friday had become Saturday, and now Saturday had slipped into Sunday, and still she'd heard nothing.

And so she fought to narrow her world down to her house, her friends, her work. And tried to forget that Rand Mitchell had ever been a part of it.

MONDAY MORNING, thought Rand, without the tiniest vestige of interest. He didn't feel as if he belonged in his own skin. The weekend had been endless, one long exercise of avoiding the phone, of watching the time crawl by and trying to convince himself that he'd get used to life without Cilla.

Someday.

He'd always grown up blithely thinking that the challenge was finding that right person, and that once you did, things fell into place. He'd never thought about how it would be if you found the right person and it just wouldn't work.

He'd lived thirty-two years without her, and now, after three months, losing her felt like losing a piece of himself. Time and again over the weekend he'd find himself making a note to tell Cilla something, or saving a story to pass along.

Only to remember that he couldn't anymore.

Sure, he could go to her and reconcile. Their current conflict would eventually fade away, but that wouldn't do anything about the real issue. The real issue was fundamentally wound up with how he fit into her world. He'd told himself over and over again that it was okay.

It wasn't, and he needed to remember that.

The other thing he needed to remember was that they had two weeks to get a business proposal finished. He massaged his temples. Launching into an affair with Cilla had been stupid to the nth degree. Sure, he could tell himself he hadn't been able to help it. Reality was he'd known that chances were they'd wind up breaking up badly, forced to work together when it was the last thing either wanted. At least in the past when he'd separated from girlfriends they'd been able to just go their separate ways.

There was a reason getting involved with colleagues was a bad move.

Nothing for it, he reminded himself, and reached out for the phone. Before he could touch the receiver, it rang.

"Mitchell."

"Rand? It's Elliot Patterson from Stratosphere Executive Search. Is this a good time?"

"I've got a few minutes," he said briefly.

"I've spoken with the client and they want to set up a meet with you. They'd like a chance to get to know you better, and vice versa. Look, do you have an afternoon free this week? We'll grab lunch, talk about plans and goals. It'll give us a chance to see if it's a good enough fit to keep discussions going."

Rand checked his Palm Pilot. "I can't clear time until Wednesday, and even then it'll only be a couple of hours."

"A couple of hours will let us know what we need to." Elliot's voice was brisk. "I can have some material couriered over today so that you can get acquainted with them. What's your home address?"

Rand told him, and made a note in his PDA. "So where's the firm located?"

"California. Offices in San Jose and L.A. If you wind up being a fit, you could work out of either, of course. So let's settle on a time for Wednesday."

Minutes later, Rand hung up the phone thoughtfully. Location hardly mattered, of course. His parents would be happy to see him stay in L.A. On the other hand, a change of scenery would probably be the best thing that could happen to him. He supposed he ought to be disappointed at the idea of a job in San Jose rather than the globe-trotting position he'd held before with Danforth, but in truth it was a relief to think about getting back to what he did best.

He'd never planned to stay with the company. He didn't belong here now. One way or another, whether the venture capitalist job worked out or not, he needed to move on.

He picked up the phone and dialed Cilla.

"Cilla Danforth."

Rand closed his eyes at the sound of her voice. "It's Rand."

A beat went by before she answered. "How are you?"

Miserable. Sorry. Wishing he could wipe away the previous week entirely.

Knowing he couldn't made his voice brusque. "We need to meet about your proposal. I've got to do some work on the European Danforth stores, so I need to know what you want from me."

Her voice was cool. "Sounds like we've got some things to talk about. Your office or mine?"

"Neither. I've booked conference room C for two o'clock." Get it over with, he thought. It was safest. "You open?"

THERE WAS A TAP on Cilla's door and her mother stood there, cool and chic in a pale gold silk pantsuit that complimented her ash blond hair. Going gray, for Elaine Danforth, had merely been an excuse to take her hair color even lighter.

She smiled now at Cilla and swept into the room. "Hello, darling," she said walking close to clasp hands and present a smoothly powdered cheek for a kiss.

"Mother." Cilla blinked in surprise. "What are you doing here?"

"I had lunch in the area. Can't I stop by the office now and again to see how you're getting on? How officious you look, behind a desk." Elaine sat back in the client chair and crossed her legs gracefully.

There were some daughters who would no doubt pour their hearts out to their mothers at a time like this. Cilla envied them. She and her mother had never been able to communicate particularly well, especially not since Cilla had begun working at Danforth. Elaine had always seen it as a defection, from mother to father. She'd never been able to understand Cilla for Cilla's sake.

"You look thinner, Cilla. Your father's working you too hard."

Cilla forced a smile and shook her head. "Hardly."

"Nonsense. You're tired. A mother can always tell. We should do something about it." Elaine paused a minute, then snapped her fingers theatrically. "I know. How about if you play hooky next week on my birthday and we can go to Elizabeth Arden for the day, just us girls, to get ready for my party."

Cilla's heart sank. The party. "I told you last month that I have a buying trip next week, Mother, remember? We're going to L'Orangerie tomorrow night. I've been looking forward to it." A white lie. Dinner with her parents was right up there with root canals.

Elaine snorted—elegantly, as always. "We own the company, darling. Just change your plans."

"We might own our company, Mother, we don't own the New York fashion houses. These are the days they can take me, so I have to go."

"Danforth clout counts for something," Elaine flared.

The legendary Danforth clout. For the thousandth time, Cilla wondered how her mother could simultaneously worship the Danforth empire and loathe it as she did. "Look, Dad and I will take you out, like we planned."

"Oh, sure, you and he are quite the team."

It was a measure of how distracted she'd been by Rand that Cilla would have made the tactical mistake of even remotely appearing to ally herself with her father. In a family where the resident couple was anything but a pair, neutral was the safest way to go. Cilla glanced at her computer clock and gathered her papers together. She stood.

"Where are you going?"

"It was lovely to see you, Mother." She came around the desk to kiss Elaine's cheek. "I've got to go to a meeting, but I'll see you tomorrow night and we'll celebrate your birthday. It'll be fun," she said with false enthusiasm. Another lie. "I'll bring you something special back from New York."

"Have a good trip, dear." For the first time, Elaine really seemed to look at her. "Are you all right? Something's wrong, isn't it?"

"Nothing's wrong," Cilla maintained. "I'm just a little stressed about this meeting. You know how business is," she added, squirming inwardly.

Elaine shook her head. "Get some rest tonight." She kissed Cilla's forehead. "You really don't look well."

"I'm fine," Cilla replied automatically.

And that was the biggest lie of all.

CILLA SET HER FILES AND her notepad on the conference room table with an impatient thump. It wasn't the palatial boardroom but a claustrophobic cube designed to seat perhaps six or eight people around a faux wood-grain table. The chairs were chrome, with thin woven pads. The walls were bare, save for a white board bearing what looked like a list of advertising campaigns with a decision next to each: hold, increase, terminate.

Terminate.

She shivered in the air-conditioning. She'd survived the weekend, but she'd missed Rand with an intensity that sliced at her. When she'd opened her eyes that morning, her first thought was that she was going to see him again. However mixed up things had been, they were going to be okay. This bobble would work itself out. One way or another, once they'd seen each other, they'd resolve their conflict.

When she'd heard Rand's flat, emotionless voice over the phone, though, she'd known something was still wrong. Everything was still wrong. He'd called instead of just walking into her office. They were meeting in the conference room.

Neutral ground, suitable for negotiations between hostile parties.

So she'd arrived early, trying not to feel embattled. They'd had other disagreements and they'd always worked them out. Once he understood why she'd done what she'd done, Rand had always been fine. That's how it would work out this time, also, she told herself, though uncertainty began uncoiling somewhere deep within her. It would be all right. It had to be.

Then Rand walked through the door and her pulse began thudding in her ears. It had only been a couple of days since she'd seen him. It seemed more like weeks.

He'd nicked himself shaving. His gray-blue shirt turned his eyes to silver, or maybe that was just his mood. It was a face she knew almost as well as her own, one she'd woken to nearly every morning for going on three months.

But his expression was closed, as though they were strangers.

He nodded to her impersonally. "Cilla."

"Rand." She began to tremble.

"Thanks for taking time to meet. I'm getting pulled off on some of the EU Danforth work beginning this week, so I wanted to find out what you need from me on your business plan. We should break down the task list and get rolling." No pleasantries, no greeting, just the abrupt jump into work.

Cilla swallowed. "How do you want to do it?"

He gave her a level look. "You should probably

make that call since you're the primary. I can make some recommendations, if you like."

"I'm not the primary. This project belongs to both of us."

"Cilla. As far as the board is concerned, this is your baby. They're expecting a proposal from you, and I'm supposed to help. So that's what I'm ready to do—help." He was remote rather than angry, and in that moment she began to understand the full extent of the damage. This wasn't going to go away. It wasn't going to be a Hollywood ending where just seeing one another would be enough.

"That's not what I want." Her voice was unsteady, and they both knew she was talking about more than the proposal.

"I'm sorry. That's the best I can do right now," he said flatly. If it hurt him to say it, it didn't show, except maybe in the tightening of his jaw.

"Rand," she pleaded, "we need to talk about this."

He looked at a point on the wall, and then at her. "I think we've talked enough."

It was like being slapped, and she blinked. As hurt as she'd been all weekend, she'd assumed that everything was ultimately going to be all right. She'd assumed that he would still be ready to try. Now, in an instant, everything had changed. She wanted to beg, she wanted to weep. Pride wouldn't let her do either, though—pride, and the closed-off look in his eyes that warned her nothing she could do would make a difference.

"We should make a shortlist of locations and get some demographics on them." His voice was toneless.

"I believe your memo mentioned Manhattan and Miami Beach."

"And London and Montreal." It took her two tries to get the words out.

She remembered the night they'd sat on her couch, flushed in the success of the Annex opening, giddy with the joy of their love affair. It had been only five weeks before, and yet it already seemed like a time captured in some golden wash of color, like an insect trapped in amber. How could they have come from that easy comfort to this frigid distance?

And how in God's name was she going to live with it?

"I'll take London." Rand made a note on his pad. "I've already done some groundwork there. I can take whatever other city you don't want. We'll need demographics, competitive assessment, real estate estimates. Do you want to draft the straw man proposal, or shall I?"

Once, they'd worked together. Now, they would be separate, meeting only occasionally to bridge the gap. "I'll do it." She squared her shoulders. "Get me your site data by Friday morning. I'll put it into the draft and have my father look it over."

Rand nodded. "I'll be out Wednesday afternoon, but it shouldn't be a problem. When do you want to meet again?"

"Friday morning."

IT WAS ABOUT the lousiest day he'd had in recent memory—rivaled only, perhaps, by the whole of the previous weekend. Rand's phone rang and he lifted the receiver. "Mitchell," he snapped.

"I leave for a week, and I only ask one thing of you, one thing. And do you do it?"

Rand paused for a moment and collected himself. "Hello, Wayne."

"You, sir, should be ashamed of yourself," his friend returned. "All I asked was that you take care of our team for four games. Four games. And what do you do?"

"Look, don't even start—"

"You let them lose three, is what you do," Wayne continued.

Rand really wasn't in the mood for this. "Clearly, I wasn't paying attention."

There was a short silence.

"Ah," said Wayne eventually. "You were distracted."

"Mmm."

"I see." There was another pause. "Do I want to know why?"

Rand didn't want to get into it, not now. He didn't think he could bear to relive the moments with Cilla. "Probably not."

"Oh." Wayne cleared his throat. "Well, thank you for sparing me."

"Don't mention it," Rand replied.

"No, I won't."

But Rand could practically hear the gears turning in Wayne's head over the phone. "I will say however, that it's time you paid more attention to your team, in person. I say it's time we sat your butt somewhere along the left-field line and reminded you about what's important in life."

Despite his mood, Rand almost smiled. "Look, I appreciate the gesture…"

"Box seats."

Wayne clearly was trying very hard. "You have box seats?"

"I could."

Rand hesitated, then thought that he needed to start getting over Cilla some time. Or, at least, be distracted from her. "All right, I'm in."

"Of course you are," Wayne said triumphantly.

Rand sighed. After all, what were friends for?

THE LAST THING SHE WANTED to do the day after her life had fallen apart was have dinner with her parents. Some people would turn to their parents first for succor. Not her. Not her parents. Navigating an evening with them was always an adventure, the endless bickering and the petty jealousies creating a backdrop of constant agitation. Still, her mother's birthday was the following week and Cilla would be gone on a buying trip. This dinner provided a means of all-important appeasement.

Now, she sat with them in the fashionable restaurant, the sniping between them grating on her like ground glass. They'd never gotten on well, for as long as she remembered, but in recent years, it seemed, it had escalated into all-out warfare.

Or maybe now she just noticed it more. It wasn't how all couples acted. She thought of Rand's parents at the triathlon, the gentle teasing, the unquestioning support, the affection that showed through in every gesture. No, some couples weren't like that at all.

"If she weren't going out of town to take care of that business of yours, she'd be around for my party," her mother was saying, still irate that she wasn't going to be feted on her birthday. She didn't take it up with Cilla, though. She wouldn't. Instead, it was another grievance to hold against her husband.

Sam Danforth bridled. "That business of mine, as you call it, is what pays for all your credit cards and vacations."

"All my vacations? Is it my fault you refuse to go anywhere that doesn't have a golf course?"

"Elaine, I work my ass off to make this company a success. When I've got time off, I want to do what I want to do."

"You're the most selfish man I've ever met, Sam Danforth."

"Me? I could take lessons from you."

Cilla sipped her wine and tried not to roll her eyes.

"Fine," Elaine sniffed. "I know when I'm not wanted. You go on your little golf holidays and I'll go to China by myself. It'll be more enjoyable without you anyway."

Cilla raised her glass, listening to the bickering go on as it had all her life. Suddenly her hand froze. Suddenly she saw the pattern. Solo. Their solution to everything was to split up and pursue their separate goals. Their pattern was to pursue what they wanted, without ever considering their partner. *Be a team player,* she remembered Rand saying. She'd lived with her parents her whole life. She'd known they'd battled. She'd always tried to ignore it, so she'd never listened enough to understand that the dialogue was always about the two of them separately.

And maybe that's what she had absorbed.

She'd been hurt that Rand hadn't been mollified by the fact that what she'd done, she'd done without thinking. To her, it made sense. To him, it wasn't justification but a statement of the problem. And for the first time, she truly got it. What he wanted was someone who integrated their partner into their life, into their thinking. She'd never intentionally shut him out, but now she saw often she'd done it out of carelessness, out of not making him a priority.

She remembered Josephine and Vinnie, always making the effort with the small courtesies, the caring, and she understood. She finally understood.

Now she just had to convince Rand.

SUN SLANTED through the blinds of the conference room, backlighting the trio of investors. Rand relaxed in his seat. As far as he was concerned, he was interviewing them even as they were interviewing him. He didn't need the job. He might want it, but only if it was right. It needed to be a fit both ways.

As far as that went, it was pretty clear that they were liking what they'd seen so far. No surprise there—this was the kind of interview he could do in his sleep, even if his heart wasn't fully in it.

"Well, I think we should keep discussions going here, Rand," said John Woodson, the head of the VC group. "What I'd really like to do is have you meet with our full investor group up in the San Jose office." Woodson looked about fifty, but was only in his late thirties, according to Rand's research. That was what bond trading did to you. Then again, it had also done other things, like setting Woodson up with enough dough to launch a company.

"Think about that biotech focus we talked about," Rand suggested. "There's a lot of strong technology out there, a lot of ways to win."

Woodson rose to shake his hand. "That's where we need the right managing partner. Elliot will be in touch."

He ought to have been truly psyched about the opportunity that had dropped in his lap, Rand thought as he got home. After a year spent fruitlessly searching for the right job, he'd just had one handed to him on a platter. It had the effect of lightening his mood a few shades from black, but that was about the extent of it. Intellectually, he knew it was right for him. Of course, intellectually he knew that getting the hell out of Dodge would put him that much closer to starting to get over Cilla.

As to actually getting over Cilla, well, one thing at a time. He changed into shorts and moved out to his balcony with a beer, staring out at the Hollywood Hills as they turned ruddy in the light of the setting sun.

The job represented a chance to move back into the world he knew, a world he loved. Running a VC firm wouldn't actually involve making anything, but he'd be intrinsic to helping others realize their dreams. He could be as involved as he wanted to be. It would give him a chance to sit on boards, help make the decisions that would help shape tomorrow's Hewlett-Packard or Microsoft. It would let him use his full array of skills.

It would let him get away from the wreckage of what he'd had with Cilla.

The regrets and memories? They'd follow him always.

CILLA STARED AT her computer screen, tabulating the data she'd accrued on Miami Beach and Montreal. The proposal was nearly together. It had taken longer than it should have to write up. Then again, it was hard to concentrate when her life was lying in a shambles around her.

The office had gradually quieted as people knocked off for the day and headed out. She'd remained, working on her document.

She'd remained, hoping for a chance to talk with Rand.

After missing the previous afternoon, he'd be working late to catch up, she was betting. And, indeed, she saw, walking into the hallway, his light was on.

Show time.

When she reached his open door, Cilla tapped on the wood and Rand looked up inquiringly. Just for a moment, before the shutters came down, she saw the person she knew. He was still in there, it was just a matter of reaching him.

She swallowed. "Got a minute?"

"Okay." His face was guarded, though he barely glanced up from his computer. "I'm just finishing up the data summaries on my sites. Check your e-mail in about half an hour."

"That's fine, but that's not what I wanted to talk about." She shut the door and walked to the client chair. Forget about nerves, she thought, she just needed to tell him that she'd finally understood. It would work out.

He stopped what he was doing, reluctantly, and looked directly at her for the first time. "Cilla, don't. We've been over this."

"No. Not what I want to talk about." She twisted her fingers together. "I've been doing some thinking about what happened Friday, about the things that you said. And you were right. I haven't been acting like part of a couple, not really. There are reasons for it, but it doesn't change the facts."

She moistened her lips. "My family wasn't like yours, growing up. My parents…they fight like cats and dogs, they always have. I just figured that was what couples were like. It's why, when I grew up, I never wanted to get serious about anyone, so I never learned. That's not an excuse, it's a reason." Her voice shuddered and she blinked rapidly to clear her eyes. Rand looked down at his desk.

"I went out with my parents the other night. Everything they talked about was each of them separately. All I heard was 'I.' There was no 'we.' They're not like your parents. You think 'we' because that's what you grew up with. I grew up with the opposite." She took an uneven breath.

"I finally really and truly understand why you've been angry with me. And I'm sorry." She fell silent. *Say something,* she thought.

His voice was low. "I haven't been angry, Cilla. I mean, I was, but there was really no point. I guess I was more…disappointed."

It gave her a surge of hope to hear it. Disappointed held open the door. Disappointed was what he'd said in the past, and he'd always been ready to give it another try.

"I get it now, Rand, in a way I didn't before." She fought not to sound overeager. "I know how it's supposed to be. Just give this another chance and I'll show you."

He just sat, watching her. Wait a minute, she thought confusedly. This was the part where he was supposed to come around the desk and hold her, say it was going to be all right.

Instead, his gaze returned to the desktop, then across the room. Finally, he looked at her again. "This is the same conversation we've had before."

It was as if she'd been sucker punched. "What do you mean? I know why now. I can change."

"Cilla, every time we've had a problem, it always ends up with you promising to do better, saying that now you get it, now you'll be better. And then we go another round and it happens again in another way." The mask had totally dropped, but the pain and weariness behind it were almost worse. "And every time it happens, I feel a little bit more like an idiot. If we do go another round, I'll feel even worse. And I'm tired of feeling that way. So no, I don't think we can try it again."

She swallowed, tightening her hands into fists. "I'm in love with you."

His eyes widened a fraction, but then the shutter came back down. "Cilla, you were talking about things you learn from your parents. One of the things I've learned from mine is that it's what you do that counts, it's not the words you say. You are who you are."

There was a screaming in her head and she blinked furiously to keep her eyes dry. "Rand, please. Don't punish us both because I've been stupid."

"I'd be punishing us both if I let it go on." Now he

did rise and come around to her. "We gave it a good go, Cilla." He pressed his lips to her forehead. "Let's just leave it at that."

SHE MANAGED TO LEAVE gracefully, for that much, Cilla could be grateful. The drive to Brentwood was merely a blur. The moments in Rand's office kept running over and over in her head as though they were on an automatic loop. *We gave it a good go, Cilla. Let's just leave it at that.* She wouldn't cry, she told herself fiercely, not until she got to her house. Like some sort of wounded creature, she wanted only to be home.

And there, she'd figure out a way to go on.

But home could do nothing to keep reality at bay. And if she finally let herself dissolve in hopeless tears, she felt no better for it. Then again, she didn't expect to. She didn't expect to for a long time.

Cilla groped for the phone. There was only one person she wanted to talk with at this point, her closest friend in all the world.

"Hello?" The voice on the phone was froggy with sleep.

"Trish? I woke you up. Never mind, go back to sleep."

"Cilla?" Trish's concern was quick and complete. "Never mind, I'm up. What's wrong? You sound terrible."

For a moment, Cilla wished with all her heart that Trish were there, just to hug and to sit with until the tempest passed.

"It's Rand." Her voice was unsteady. "We broke up." It started her crying afresh, and she groped for a tissue.

"Tell me what happened," Trish said gently, and Cilla did, going back to all of the days leading up to that night. It was nearly unbearable to revisit it, would have been unbearable with anyone but Trish, with her calm, empathetic acceptance.

"So it's over," Cilla finished. "I just don't know how to get past it, Trish, God help me I really don't."

"Do you love him?"

"Yes."

"Did you tell him?"

It sent her back into tears. She'd told him and it hadn't mattered to him at all.

"He loves you, Cilla, you know that, don't you? No matter what's happened, he loves you. Otherwise this wouldn't have mattered so much."

"Then why doesn't he give me another chance?"

"Maybe he doesn't know how. You know the bumps that Ty and I had to go through before we got things figured out," Trish reminded her. "It's not always easy. Give him time, like Ty gave to me."

"But Ty didn't have to see you every day." Cilla squeezed her eyes tightly shut. "Trish, I don't know how I'm going to get through it as it is. I mean, I've got to work with him every day. I don't know how I'm going to do it."

"You're strong, Cilla." Trish's voice was steady. "You'll find a way."

"I don't feel very strong right now."

"No one ever does in the middle of the night."

At the sound of Trish's stifled yawn, Cilla looked at the clock. "God, what am I thinking of? It's two in the morning where you are."

"Doesn't matter."

"Of course it matters. Don't you movie people start at the crack of dawn?"

"So? Sleep's for losers. I want to be sure that you're okay."

"I'm as okay as I'm going to be. Go to sleep," Cilla ordered.

"Call me tomorrow?"

"Yeah. Sweet dreams, honey. Thanks for being there."

"Anytime," Trish said, her voice already muffled with sleep.

Sleep might have helped Cilla, but she was too keyed up for it. Drinking? Drinking was something you did for fun; it wasn't her brand of oblivion. So she watched the hours go by, dreading the morning, dreading the absence of hope.

Dreading the prospect of seeing Rand again.

In the end, she showered and dressed as the sun was rising, trying to camouflage the ravages of the night with makeup. No makeup could disguise the hollowness in her eyes, though.

At 6:00 a.m., the office was silent, a balm for her wounded feelings. And so she worked on the proposal, polishing it, even as she weighed her options.

By midmorning, she'd finished her draft and printed it out. To say that she settled on what to do as she saw the sheets come out of the printer was overcomplicating things; she'd known when she'd left the office the night before the only tenable choice.

She went to her father's office.

He was free to see her, which in and of itself was a rarity. He was in a bad mood, which was not.

"What do you want, Cilla?"

"A couple minutes of your time."

"You're in my office, aren't you?"

She approached his desk. "Here's the business plan for the Annex chain. It's just a draft, but we wanted to get your comments on it before the final version goes to the board."

He took it when she handed it to him. It was hard, so hard to say the words. Then again, not saying them would be even harder. "I want off the Annex project," she blurted. He just stared at her. "It's running well. I think I need to pay more attention to my buying right now."

He slapped his hands down on the desk. "All right, what is going on here?" He cursed, shaking his head. "I've seen a lot of things in my time. Plenty of people jumping off dog projects, people leaving boot prints on one another's backs they're rushing so fast. I've never seen people fighting to get off a winner."

Cilla blinked. "What do you mean?" She hadn't expected him to be thrilled, and she probably needed to have her head examined, but it was the only answer. "I'm just making a simple request."

Her father's face looked like thunder. "Who the hell is going to run this thing if you're all bailing out right and left?" he demanded.

"Rand can take it from here. He's got it well in hand."

Her father snorted. "Hardly. Mitchell's off the project. He was in here an hour ago."

"For what?" she asked, stunned.

"Tendering his resignation."

19

IT WAS AMAZING to Rand that Silicon Valley could be so hot in venture circles and yet look so pedestrian. The predominant architecture was concrete Tilt-Up, usually painted in fetching earth tones. Industrial area blended into industrial area, San Jose blended into Santa Clara which blended into Mountain View. Silicon Valley was a crucible of high tech, but it could never be accused of style.

Rand sat in the ninth-floor conference room at Future Technology Ventures, watching planes take off and land at the San Jose airport and waiting. Throughout the morning and early afternoon, he'd had meetings with most of the staff. The long working lunch with the investors had felt more like a strategy meeting than an interview. Now, he waited and amused himself by guessing how much the company paid for offices in one of the few area high-rises.

"Rand, good to see you again."

John Woodson walked into the room, filling it immediately with his energy the same way a good stand-up comedian claimed a stage. It was a good sign, Rand figured. Woodson had brought him up to San Jose to trot him out in front of the remaining investment

partners and to see if he played nice with the other kids.
It was the way Rand would have handled hiring him if
he'd been in Woodson's spot: choose a handful of candidates he liked, try them out on the rest of the company and investors, but keep the final call to himself.

If Rand were a betting man, he'd say he'd made the
short list the week before and was one of two or three
Woodson-approved candidates who were getting the
look-see.

And he was about to move onto a shorter list still.
He rose and put out his hand. "John."

Woodson shook hands and dropped into a chair. "I
hear you've had a busy morning. Sorry I couldn't join
you for the lunch with the partners, but it sounds like
things went well. So what do you think of our team?"

Here it came, Rand thought. The dance had begun.
"I think you've made some good moves, but it's time
for you to make it to the next level. The market's ready
for it."

And he was ready for it, too. Rand wondered what
Woodson would think if he knew that Rand had already
quit Danforth. Somehow, he had a feeling that Woodson would respect it. You were either engaged in the
work or you weren't, and if you weren't, there wasn't
much reason for sticking around unless you needed a
paycheck. Rand didn't, at least not for six or eight
months. With the uptick in the market, he'd gambled
that if Woodson didn't give him a job, someone else
would.

Woodson studied him. "Things are getting ready to
take off. And I want you at the helm when it does."

There it was, out on the table. Woodson appeared to

be the variety of manager who knew what he wanted and wasn't tentative about recognizing it. Then again, you didn't get to be a top bond trader without a firm grip on the human psyche, above all.

It was all coming together.

He had to escape Danforth, pure and simple. He had to get away from the memories that reproached him at every turn. He knew the decision to resign had been right, for him, for Cilla, for the two of them together. Why, then, couldn't he forget the stricken look on her face, a face that had thinned visibly in a matter of days? He'd never been a cruel man. In his gut, he was certain that stretching out what they'd been doing would ultimately be crueler. And yet…

And yet he still loved her, and that was nothing that was going to go away anytime soon. But Woodson didn't want to hear about all that. Woodson was waiting for an answer, and Rand needed to move into his future.

"I think it's an interesting opportunity," Rand said. "I'd like to hear more."

Woodson's mouth twitched. "And just how much of the more is it going to take to get you?"

This was a man he could work with, Rand thought suddenly, and for the first time he truly relaxed. "Let's talk about that."

EDISON FIELD was a sea of noise and color as the Angels played the Indians. Rand remembered as a kid, sitting up on the third level, bringing his glove religiously as though a ball might by some miraculous chance make it up to the nosebleed sections. Now, he and

Wayne stretched out in the high-priced boxes, along the third base line.

The Angels ran onto the field for the start of the fourth inning, their uniforms very white against the ruddy clay and emerald grass of the field.

"So the VC opening's looking good, huh?"

"So far. Looks like I'll be working out of San Jose, though they've got an office down here."

"That's why you're looking like such a sad sack, because you're going to have to be apart from your girlfriend."

"I'm not looking like a sad sack," Rand muttered. "And Cilla and I split up."

"I thought something was up with you. When'd that happen?"

"A week or so ago."

Wayne nodded slowly. "Hence the job shift."

"The job shift is a good career move."

"And quitting Danforth before you had something solid in place, was that a good career move, too?" Wayne flagged the hot dog vendor as he walked past.

"Danforth was something to fill up an empty slot on the résumé," Rand said, taking the dogs Wayne handed him. "The market's coming back. Even if this VC thing goes south, I'll find something."

"In the meantime, scoffing a paycheck to go places like Milan wouldn't have been all bad," Wayne pointed out.

Rand scowled. "I wasn't going to Milan anymore, remember? I was stuck here in L.A."

"Oh, yeah, that's right. Working on that special project with Cilla, your no-longer girlfriend." Wayne doctored his dog with mustard and took a thoughtful bite. "Well, you said that maybe working together and being involved would be a bad combination. No matter how stuck on someone you are, I guess it loses something once you're seeing them every waking minute."

"That wasn't the problem," Rand said around his hot dog. They'd had their challenges professionally, perhaps, but Cilla was a good partner. Her judgment was solid and she didn't shirk work. More, she was easy to be with, quick to laugh, slow to take offense. And that was just the Cilla by day. Cilla by night brought a whole new set of pleasures.

Now, he couldn't figure out which was harder, seeing her or not seeing her. He'd thought getting away from her would get her off his mind, but she'd been in New York for the week and all he'd done was stare at her darkened office and think of her.

"So if working together wasn't the problem, what was? I thought she was the überbabe to beat all überbabes."

"She was." Rand set down his hot dog, appetite suddenly gone.

"Did she suddenly turn psycho?"

Rand watched the pitcher shake off signs from the catcher until he had the one he wanted. "No. She was great."

"I can definitely understand why you gave her the boot. She sounds like a regular pain in the ass."

"Look, we had problems, okay? She wasn't a team player."

Wayne winced as if he had an earache. "Wasn't a team player? That's what the second baseman out there says to the outfielder, not what you say to your girl-friend."

"I told you about her doing stuff on the project without telling me."

"Do you need to be told everything?"

"I need to be kept in the loop," Rand stated, feeling fresh irritation.

"Well, did she screw up or did her decisions work out?"

"That's not the point."

"That's right, it's probably your control-freak thing that's the point." Wayne finished his second hot dog and crumpled the napkins up into a wad.

"What's that supposed to mean?" Rand demanded.

"Sounds like you want to be running the show and you're ticked that she's not letting you."

"It wasn't just work, it was stuff between us."

"Yeah, so? Nobody gets it dead-on just out of the gate. Eckstein out there made an error last night. Do you see them kicking him off the team?"

"Look, after a while, you're supposed to get it, aren't you?"

"Well, there's a while and then there's a while. What does she say?"

Abruptly, Rand's anger dropped away, leaving only emptiness. "She's sorry. That she understands where I'm coming from now."

"And does she?"

"I don't know," he said simply. "That's the point."

"So why did you break up with her if you don't know."

Rand stared out at the field but he was seeing Cilla's face as she told him she loved him. "I don't know."

And so they watched the game and Rand brooded.

By the bottom of the ninth, the Angels were behind but attempting a rally when the designated hitter came up.

"Oh, perfect, this is just what we need," Wayne groaned.

Normally a strong bat, the DH was currently mired in a record slump that had been the talk of the sports news. He was the last person a fan wanted to see at the plate.

"He's going to whiff or hit into a double play," Wayne predicted, shaking his head as the DH knocked the first pitch foul for a strike. "They should have taken him out and put someone else in."

"Who? The guys on the bench are there for a reason." Rand stared intently at the batter's box, his body tense.

"The batboy could do a better job."

"He's the team's best guy," Rand maintained as another pitch blew by the plate for strike two.

Wayne grimaced. "Not right now."

The pitcher waited for the sign and set. "Look, when your best guy's slumping, you don't sit him down," Rand argued. "You stay behind him, let him work—" He stopped abruptly, realizing what he'd just said.

The pitcher kicked and threw. "You let him work it out," Rand said slowly as the DH stepped into the pitch and swung, sending it arcing far, far out over the field and into the grandstands.

"You give him another chance."

THE PROBLEM WITH business trips, Cilla thought as she plodded across the Danforth parking garage to her car, was that when you got home all the work was still waiting for you. It wasn't as if elves came out at night and did it while you were gone. Nope, you got home and you worked late, just like she had this night. Still, working late had one benefit, she thought as she yawned and imagined dropping into bed. Maybe for once she'd be able to sleep instead of lying awake with her mind full of thoughts of Rand and what-ifs.

What-ifs were profitless. Some mistakes you couldn't come back from. If nothing else, at least she'd learned that. Soon, he'd be gone and maybe she could start the process of forgetting.

She shook her head at the thought. It was like telling a blind person to forget that they'd once been able to see. She'd never be able to forget. The best she might achieve would be to accept it and go forward.

Cilla punched the unlock button on her key as she skirted around her car to reach the driver's side. It wasn't until she got in that she noticed the tilt.

A tilt she remembered from the highway in the desert.

And her with no spare. With a groan, she brought her hands up to cover her face. She'd known she needed to get a new spare after her adventure in the desert, and she'd meant to. The problem was that she'd always seemed to have something going.

So here it was, after eight on a Friday night and she had a flat tire and no solution. At least Triple A wouldn't take two hours to get to her, but what the heck were they going to do when they got there? A headache began throbbing in her temples. All she wanted was to get home.

There was a knock at her window. "Need some help?"

And she turned to see Rand. He looked thinner and a little tired and utterly delicious.

And he was smiling.

Hope sprinted through her. She rolled down the window. "Hi."

"Hi. Looks like you've got a problem."

A flat tire wasn't a problem. Losing the man you loved was a problem. "I was thinking about calling a tow truck."

"Really?" He walked up to the side of her car. "Not thinking about changing it yourself, huh?"

A chance, she thought, just a chance to make it right was all they needed. "I'd rather work with someone on that."

"You could team up with me, if you wanted to." Rand opened her car door.

"I can't think of anything I'd rather do more." And then she launched herself into his arms.

He caught her to him. "God, Cilla, I've been going nuts without you. I was an idiot and I'm sorry," he murmured.

She pressed her face into his shoulder, absorbing the marvelous, wonderful, stupendous reality of him. "I missed you, I missed you so much. I'm sorry I screwed everything up."

"You didn't." He pulled away and looked down at her. "Stuff happens in relationships. You talk it over and you get over it. My mistake was not listening, and wanting everything to happen on my timeline. That's not how it works." He framed her face with his hands.

"I love you," she whispered. "I meant it when I said it the other night. I knew it the night of the reception but I was afraid of it. I was—"

"I love you, too. I knew it weeks ago. I never said it to you and I should have."

She stared at him in wonder. "Say it again," she murmured.

"I love you." And he lowered his mouth to hers.

The kiss flowed through her, buoying her up on a rising tide of joy. With this, there was nothing that they couldn't overcome.

Cilla raised her head to look at him. "I know more now, Rand. I've learned from it, and I'm going to do better from now on."

"We both are. I want you in my life, forever. I couldn't stand to lose you again."

"You won't have to."

He held her for a long, long time, saying nothing. At first, the closeness was enough, but gradually, the heat of his body against hers raised flickers of desire.

And she could feel what it did to him in return.

Finally, Rand stirred. "Let's get out of here," he said impatiently. "We've got some making up to do."

"Well, there's a little matter of a flat tire to deal with first," Cilla told him.

"Flat tire?" He reached into his coat pocket and brought out a canister of compressed air. "What flat tire?"

And she laughed and pulled him close.

Epilogue

A WARM BREEZE whispered through the trees, teasing the white tablecloths, sending the strings of Chinese lanterns dancing. Vases of camellias on the long tables smelled sweetly of summer. The ceremony was long over, the celebration winding down to loosened ties and cast off shoes, relaxing and spending time with friends.

Rand's fingers wound around Cilla's.

"Happy?" he murmured to her, playing with the ring on her left hand.

"As happy as I can ever remember being." She leaned over to kiss him.

And the diamond flashed in the lantern light.

"I swear," a voice said over their heads, "people get engaged and it's just public displays of affection everywhere you go." Delaney stood behind them, arms crossed, shaking her head. "Another one bites the dust," she said sadly, gesturing down the table.

Sabrina looked up from where she stood, dressed in an absolutely simple column of ivory, her hair crowned with a circlet of creamy white Madagascar jasmine. "I heard that."

"As well you should. You were our first defector. I'm blaming your example for Cilla and Trish and Kelly. It's a wonder there are any of us single at all."

"Trish and Kelly are still single, remember?" Kelly called from where she leaned against Kev.

"Technicalities," Delaney responded. "You're the next best thing to hitched, unlike us swinging single girls."

"Methinks the lady doth protest too much," Thea said mildly, looking over from where she was chatting with Paige and another of her interchangeable innocuous men.

Delaney flapped a hand dismissively. "I'll get to it when I get to it. Trish and Kelly are done deals. My bet's on you next."

Thea snorted. "In your dreams. I say it'll be her," she said pointing at Paige, who merely rolled her eyes.

"Anyone care to wager?" Delaney asked.

"I thought you were trumpeting the glories of the single life." Stef gathered Sabrina into his lap, pressing a kiss on her temple.

"Sure, but I don't mind a little profit taking. I'm making book. I'm betting that by the time Cilla and Rand get married in a year or so, we're going to lose a few more soldiers."

"And I'm betting that you're going to be first on the list," Kelly wagered.

"Put your money down, ladies and gentlemen, I'm happy to take it," Delaney said genially. "In the meantime, a toast to Cilla and Rand for giving me the opportunity."

Cilla rose. "Better yet, a toast to all of us. To the best

of friends and the best of times." She smiled down at Rand. "I wouldn't have had it any other way."

"To the Supper Club," they chorused and raised their glasses.

* * * * *

Look for the rest of the
SEX & SUPPER CLUB

Coming Summer 2006
From Harlequin Blaze

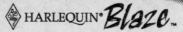

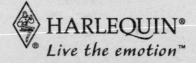

If you enjoyed what you just read,
then we've got an offer you can't resist!

Take 2 bestselling love stories FREE!

Plus get a FREE surprise gift!

Clip this page and mail it to Harlequin Reader Service®

IN U.S.A.	**IN CANADA**
3010 Walden Ave.	P.O. Box 609
P.O. Box 1867	Fort Erie, Ontario
Buffalo, N.Y. 14240-1867	L2A 5X3

YES! Please send me 2 free Blaze™ novels and my free surprise gift. After receiving them, if I don't wish to receive anymore, I can return the shipping statement marked cancel. If I don't cancel, I will receive 4 brand-new novels each month, before they're available in stores! In the U.S.A., bill me at the bargain price of $3.99 plus 25¢ shipping and handling per book and applicable sales tax, if any*. In Canada, bill me at the bargain price of $4.47 plus 25¢ shipping and handling per book and applicable taxes**. That's the complete price and a savings of at least 10% off the cover prices—what a great deal! I understand that accepting the 2 free books and gift places me under no obligation ever to buy any books. I can always return a shipment and cancel at any time. Even if I never buy another book from Harlequin, the 2 free books and gift are mine to keep forever.

150 HDN DZ9K
350 HDN DZ9L

Name	(PLEASE PRINT)
Address	Apt.#
City	State/Prov. Zip/Postal Code

Not valid to current Harlequin Blaze™ subscribers.

Want to try two free books from another series?
Call 1-800-873-8635 or visit www.morefreebooks.com.

* Terms and prices subject to change without notice. Sales tax applicable in N.Y.
** Canadian residents will be charged applicable provincial taxes and GST.
  All orders subject to approval. Offer limited to one per household.
  ® and ™ are registered trademarks owned and used by the trademark owner and or its licensee.

BLZ04R   ©2004 Harlequin Enterprises Limited.

The world's bestselling romance series.

Seduction and Passion Guaranteed!

They're the men who have everything—except a bride....

Wealth, power, charm—what else could a heart-stoppingly
handsome tycoon need? In the GREEK TYCOONS
miniseries you have already been introduced to some
gorgeous Greek multimillionaires who are in need of wives.

THE GREEK BOSS'S DEMAND
by *Trish Morey*
On sale January 2005, #2444

THE GREEK TYCOON'S
CONVENIENT MISTRESS
by *Lynne Graham*
On sale February 2005, #2445

THE GREEK'S
SEVEN-DAY SEDUCTION
by *Susan Stephens*
On sale March 2005, #2455

Pick up a Harlequin Presents® novel and you will enter a world
of spine-tingling passion and provocative, tantalizing romance!

Available wherever Harlequin books are sold.